"No, I think that Houdini's evidence is pretty conclusive."

"That doesn't mean I can't believe in ghosts myself," she said with some heat. "After all, he is—"

"Was," Brad interrupted.

"Damn you," she muttered under her breath. "He was my husband. We had a wonderful marriage."

"Did you, now? Did you really?"

Emily shivered. He meant something, but she was just not sure what it was. His arm tightened around her shoulders. She moved an inch or two more in his direction until her head was firmly on his shoulder. It wasn't the warmth that held her, but rather an undefined feeling of comfort and security. When he tilted her chin up with his big index finger she was prepared for the kiss that followed. Ready and yearning for the contact, the emotion, the glorious satisfaction.

EMMA GOLDRICK describes herself as a grandmother first and an author second. She was born and raised in Puerto Rico, where she met her husband, a career military man from Massachusetts. His postings took them all over the world, which often led to mishaps—such as the Christmas they arrived in Germany before their furniture. Emma uses the places she's been as backgrounds for her books, but just in case she runs short of settings, this prolific author and her husband are always making new travel plans.

Books by Emma Goldrick

HARLEQUIN PRESENTS

HARLEQUIN ROMANCE

Don't miss any of our special offers. Write to us at the following address for information on our newest releases.

Harlequin Reader Service
P.O. Box 1397, Buffalo, NY 14240
Canadian address: P.O. Box 603,
Fort Erie, Ont. L2A 5X3

EMMA GOLDRICK

Spirit of Love

Harlequin Books

TORONTO • NEW YORK • LONDON
AMSTERDAM • PARIS • SYDNEY • HAMBURG
STOCKHOLM • ATHENS • TOKYO • MILAN
MADRID • WARSAW • BUDAPEST • AUCKLAND

Harlequin Presents first edition April 1993
ISBN 0-373-11545-8

Original hardcover edition published in 1992
by Mills & Boon Limited

SPIRIT OF LOVE

CHAPTER ONE

As ONE drove out of Taunton on Briggs Street the intervals became more frequent than the houses, and when you got to Emily Sturtevant's place there was nothing to be seen except the old mansion up the hill next door, and a swatch of fields and trees and shrubbery. Which explained why Em rushed to the front door and peered out into the autumn sunshine when the procession went by. A limousine and an ambulance, and a hatful of noise that even the crows wouldn't believe. The birds scattered, leaving behind a cawing complaint. Em went out onto the porch. She wasn't being nosy, just neighborly, as one was in southeastern Massachusetts. And she was tired. A long nursing case had come to a sad end, all with no good result. Her head ached.

It wasn't a conversation going on up the road there. It was more like a small riot. A wheelchair appeared behind the ambulance. The two white-coated attendants maneuvered a man out into the chair. Em shaded her eyes with her hand, but could hardly make out his features. Her cat Sheba, a compact twelve-pound outdoor animal, came wandering up from the barn to stand at her side. Em scratched at the ear Sheba presented for that purpose. A ragged-edged ear. Sheba was not a peace-loving cat. Coal black, except for that tiny diamond of white in the middle of her forehead, and lovable only on her own terms. Em sat down on the top step, sweeping her skirts up beneath her. Rob liked her in skirts, so she wore pants only while working at the hospital, or out

5

on private nursing cases. Sheba stretched out beside her and rested a rounded nose in her lap.

One rotund but well-dressed woman got out of the limousine and, with the help of the two men from the ambulance, seemed to surround the wheelchair. The conversation ran the gamut from whispers to shouts. The woman shook her fingers under the seated man's nose. He growled at her, fiercely enough to send her back a step or two. The driver came out of the limousine, a young thin person who hesitantly tried to enter the fray. The two medical aides added a word or two now and then. And on it went, until Em's little ears turned red. There were several four-letter words being used repetitiously. The man in the chair hunched himself down, as if dodging a firestorm.

"Poor man," Em told Sheba. "Relatives, I'll bet." The cat muttered agreement. And then suddenly the group, some hundred yards away, became silent. Em came up to a half crouch.

"I want," yelled the man in the wheelchair, "what I told you before! I want the bunch of you to pack up and get out of here!" A resonant deep voice. It was hard to see how big he was, but a voice that size *had* to have a big body behind it. There seemed to be an echo—"out of here."

The woman began to sob. "And don't rush back," the injured man added. "Start now. I can't stand weeping women."

"You mean you can't stand women," she screamed at him, and then she turned and ran for her limousine. The men hesitated, and then joined the retreat. The procession reformed. The sleek black vehicle circled and started back toward town. As Em watched, the elderly woman in the back seat of the limousine was arguing fiercely with the driver. So much so that the vehicle swerved a couple of times on the slick road.

The ambulance attendants had been standing on the sidelines as the argument went on. Now they came back, made some adjustments to the wheelchair, and pushed it up the ramp on to the porch. Another discussion, too quiet to be heard. The ambulance driver raised his right hand in a semisalute. Both attendants went back to their vehicle, climbed in, and drove off, leaving the man in his wheelchair sitting there all by himself in the gathering twilight.

"Dear God," Em whispered. Sheba whined, stared at the other house for a moment, and then wheeled and went back to the barn, where she had a date with a field-mouse. Em watched, unable to believe what she was seeing. Why would any self-respecting bunch of people abandon an invalid on the porch of a house so far out of town?

She shook her head, and the auburn hair confined in her ponytail swung around her. She had just finished up on a long private case, but no amount of nursing had been helpful to Mrs. McCloud. After ten days the hospital had given up, the doctor had given up, and finally, in the early hours of this morning, Mrs. McCloud had given up. All of which had brought Emily back home to do her accumulated washing, give the downstairs rooms a quick once-over. Now her hair needed a good scrubbing. She took one more look at the man slumped in the wheelchair, and went back inside to do that last chore.

It took some time to finish the job. Rob liked her hair long; nursing required otherwise. So normally she bustled around with her hair bundled up in a chignon at the back of her neck. Now she luxuriated under the hot shower, tugging the pins out, letting her hair fall to her waist as she lathered and scrubbed. The freckles across the base of her snub nose refused to be washed away; she had been trying that trick since she was six years old. The thought gave her a start—twenty-one years ago. Was that possible? Four years since—— Oh, God, why can't I forget?

Half blinded, she stumbled out of the shower and swathed herself in a warm bath towel. Her reflection in the full-length mirror hanging on the back of the door taunted her. Five feet six in her bare feet. Strongly muscled shoulders; nursing often required more muscle than brains. Full breasts—Rob loved those, too. Green eyes. Narrow waist, comfortable hips. A fine figure of a woman, she told herself, all going to waste!

"This is no time to feel sorry for yourself, Emily Sturtevant," she chided, and made quick work with the towel.

Sheba came back into the house through the cat door in the kitchen. The animal waited impatiently for her, thumping her heavy tail on the worn wooden floor. "All right, supper's coming," Emily promised as she bustled around the kitchen. Through the window she could just see the edge of the porch of the house next door. Clouds were coming up, covering all but the sharp points of the sun. And the man, whoever he was, was still hunched down in that chair on the porch!

"Damn," Em snapped. "He can't stay out there. Especially if it rains!"

Sheba grumbled selfishly the minute that Em's hands ceased to move in the direction of the canned cat food.

"All right," she admonished sarcastically. "It's coming. You're welcome." Her cat ignored the conversation. Sheba was not a cat many people could love. She fitted perfectly the mood and description of an "attack cat," and she and Em had an understanding. Em moved back to the can opener, still looking out of the window. One of her fingers was immediately pinched by the can opener. She offered a few words she had learned while studying nursing, dumped the can's contents into Sheba's dish, and set it down on the floor. Her nipped finger showed no blood. With blatant disregard for all her technical knowledge, she stuck the finger into her mouth and sucked on it for comfort.

"Now, I'm going up to see about this man," she lectured her cat. Sheba, whose nose was deep into the dish, flicked a disdainful eyebrow, and continued chomping away.

"Yeah," Em chortled. "I can see how sympathetic you are." She was still laughing as the front screen door slammed behind her. To her surprise her cat had followed after her, barely missing being nipped by the door. A gust of wind tugged at Em's long skirt and sent it swirling up around her knees. A pile of red-gold maple leaves which had been collecting at the foot of the stairs all week were swept up in the same little whirlwind and sent scurrying down the street to mix with the red oak leaves. Em took time for a deep breath, a good look around, and then marched up the hill to the other house.

Bradley Colson heard the footsteps swishing through the loose leaves, and the hesitant cough from the foot of the stairs. His head ached more than his broken foot. He ran a hand through his short black hair and turned to glare. "And just who the hell are you? The welcoming committee?" And then he spied Sheba, who had just landed on Em's shoulder. "Or the local witch with her *familiar*?"

Em was about to make a smart remark when a thought struck her. She had seen that sort of look before, on the face of a wolf with one leg caught in a steel trap, unable to get away, unwilling to surrender, baring his teeth and inviting the world to *try* to attack him. This man had that same look. His eyes were narrowed. Coal black eyes, seemingly flecked with specks of gold. Impossible, of course, but there he was. His square mouth was set in anger at the world. He'll bite if you get too close, she told herself. His short military-cut hair stood straight up.

"No tongue?" he asked sarcastically. "You must be the most wonderful woman in the world if you can't talk. Come to spend the night with me?" His foot was aching madly, his temper was barely two points below explosion, and here was this . . . girl . . . to poke and pry into his life. Lovely hair. Straight and shiny as silk, blowing in the wind. But this certainly isn't my day for females, he thought.

She came up one stair, close enough to see clearly, far enough away to be beyond touch. "I'm just a neighbor," she said as she rested one hand on her hip and looked him over.

Lovely voice, he added to his inventory list. Magnificent hair, a soft contralto voice. A heart-shaped sort of face. Freckles. Not exactly beautiful, but you wouldn't have to tuck a paper bag over her head on a date. Nothing like the women who usually hounded him.

"So what do you want, just-a-neighbor? May I expect the rest of the busybodies to snoop around any minute now?"

"Rest of them?" Her face was solemn, but he could see the twinkle in her green eyes.

"Rest of the neighbors," he grumbled.

"No such luck. I'm the whole neighborhood," she said, chuckling.

"Well, I'm glad I've met you," he snapped, and tried to turn away from her. The front wheel of the chair stuck on an uneven plank in the floor of the porch. "Don't let me keep you from anything important."

"You are probably the nastiest man I've run into this year," she commented. "And, believe me, after eight years of nursing I've seen a bundle of them. When do I get to see the good side?"

"This *is* my good side," he grumbled. "What you see is what you get, lady. But I'm having trouble keeping up all this pleasantry. Why don't you go away—very quickly?"

"I can't do that. I'm a nurse."

"Oh, a nurse? I might have known. The dregs of the female race. Is it true that during your training they transfuse all your blood and substitute ice water?"

"Yes, well, you're entitled to your opinion," Em told him. I won't let him get my goat. He's trying to drive me away, or make me explode, she thought. And I'm darned if some mere man is going to get away with that! "My name is Emily. Emily Sturtevant. And in about fifteen minutes, Mr. . . ."

He glared up at her, and refused to fill in his name. She had never seen a man before with jet black eyes and thick hair in a butch cut. Soft black hair? One of her fingers reached out involuntarily and checked. Soft black hair! At least he's sitting up straight, she told herself. Look at him! A majestic wreck of a man!

"And in about fifteen minutes?"

"In about fifteen minutes there's going to be rain-storm that you wouldn't believe. I could hardly stay home without offering you some advice."

"So now you're also the weather girl?"

"I've lived here all my life. Would you like me to push you inside? There's a threshold at the door that'll make it difficult for you to do it yourself."

"I can make it." He wheeled the chair around so his back was to her, and straightened up even further. His shoulders bulged; his arms appeared to be made of oak. Only his legs—or leg?—could not handle his weight.

Em stood at the top of the stairs and watched. He propelled the chair across to the heavy old door, and fumbled with a key. Twice he dropped it, straining against the chair constraints to pick it up again. Finally the old door yielded and swung open. She could hear his sigh of relief.

He rested for a moment, and then assailed the threshold, head first. Two tries, without success. He considered for a moment, then reversed the chair and tried to bump over the blockade backward. The chair teetered, and looked as if it might tip over. Trying to be as casual as one might, Em sauntered across the porch and reached for the handles, steadying the machine. He growled at her, and hunched down in the chair again.

"Look," she said, "you don't know me or my friends, and I don't know you or your friends. Under the circumstances wouldn't it be pretty silly to get yourself soaked just for pride's sake? I can have you inside in a jiffy. Then I can go home with my conscience cleared, and you can be all alone and high and dry and curse me all you want to. Bargain?"

He made no verbal answer, but at the moment her hand touched the chair he stiffened, throwing his shoulders back, radiating all the dynamic power of his negative personality. And then he began to crumple again, slumping down with his chin against his chest in the body language of surrender.

That was the moment that Sheba surprised them both. The cat moved around to the front of the wheelchair, inspected the slumped form, then vaulted up into the man's lap, stretched out, and began to purr.

"What the hell...?" he muttered. His hand moved as if to brush the cat off, then stopped in midstroke and began to toy with Sheba's bent ear.

Two of a kind, Emily told herself, fighting down the brief touch of jealousy. After all, Sheba was *her* cat. Her practiced hands turned the chair to fit the door, and with one snap pulled it up over the threshold and into the long dark hallway. In fact, she applied too much strength, and the chair bounced and swerved. Her hand searched the nearby wall and found the light switch. As she flicked it on she thought she heard a sob from him. With the coming of the light his face was frozen in a rictus of pain. But by the time she took a second look he had smothered his reaction. They stared at each other.

He is big, Em thought, a bulk of a man, with a tanned square face and a cleft chin. If he were standing he would top six feet with ease. A grave man, in some pain from the movement. And what in God's name could his trouble be? And why did he drive away those other... relatives?

She is concerned, he thought as he tried to shut off all the pain signals shooting up his leg. I thought she might be just another one of those—but she isn't. A fair-size plain girl. Plainspoken? No beauty, this one. And a wedding ring on her finger? For some reason the ring bothered him.

"Brad," he muttered. "My name is Bradley Colson." Out of the corner of his eye he watched for the inevitable reaction. The Colson name was synonymous with money. In fact, his grandfather had been elected treasurer of the commonwealth many years earlier on the thesis that since he already had all the money in the world he wouldn't be tempted to steal the state's assets. Little did they know.

"I'm pleased to meet you." Again the soft contralto voice.

"The hell you are." Gruff, he told himself. Too gruff. You could at least be apologetic. Now what will she say?

She said nothing. She stood behind him, her fingers still touching the handles of the chair. For a moment he had the wild idea that she was bending over him. He even concocted the thought that she had brushed the top of his head with a kiss. It was a silly idea. She sighed, and he heard her make for the door.

"No. Wait." He whirled his chair around, but the front door had already closed behind her, and he hadn't the nerve to yell after her—just to make an apology. Colsons never apologized. That's what his grandfather had pounded into him through the years of his boyhood. Never apologize. He shook his head disgustedly and turned the chair toward the kitchen. It had been his grandfather's house and he knew it well. What the hell have I done? he asked himself. Come home to hide in the house of the damn tyrant who's responsible for all this?

Emily hurried down the hill, but not quickly enough. Sheba had already zipped by her at full speed, and was waiting mockingly in the shelter of the porch. The storm broke when she was halfway between the houses. The raindrops were big and cold, and once or twice they stung like hail. By the time she had slammed her own front door behind her she was soaked to the skin. Sheba sat superciliously cleaning her paws, acting unconcerned, when Em knew darn well the animal was terrified by thunderstorms.

"It's all right." She knelt and gathered the shaking animal in both arms. "It's all right. C'mon, let's get you dried off." So up the stairs again, woman and cat, and into the bathroom. She had three clean towels left. Two for Sheba, one for herself.

What you need, she told herself, is another hot shower. Her New England conscience objected. Two showers in two hours? A smile played across her lips. And why not, as long as I've paid for the heat?

Sheba curled up on the floor rug and watched as Em stripped, dashed into the shower, and disappeared in a cloud of steam. Em welcomed that steam, dancing around to keep from being scalded, but unwilling to turn on the cold water. And as she danced she pondered.

Bradley Colson. Somehow the name seemed familiar. In the newspaper, perhaps? But for the last month she had been completely immersed in Mrs. McCloud and her problems, and hadn't even had a chance to check the comic section. Bradley Colson. It would come to her if she continued to harass her mind like this. On the other hand, she thought, if I just let it lie I'll probably forget him and his ugly expressions, and be able to get about my business. Colson? Hadn't it been a Colson family who had lived in that other house when Em was a child? The family about which Gran had always said, "Keep away from that sort, child. They'll steal your eyeteeth."

And because Em had no idea which of her teeth were the eyes it had proved a very effective deterrent. Bradley Colson? Of all the list of mean men in the world, Brad Colson was probably the class leader in a business group that would rape, plunder and pillage.

"But what's it all mean?" Emily asked Sheba. "If I were hunting for a man it might be important. But I'm not."

Her cat looked up at her as if she didn't believe a word, and then slumped back down on the rug. Emily dried herself off, happy that the mirror was steamed over. It would be too much to have to stare at her nudity again.

And so into her robe, and slowly back downstairs, to prepare a simple supper.

The storm raged for an hour or more, blotting out the normally gentle twilight. It shook the old house, rattled a few shutters, and caused Sheba to attach herself to Emily as if glued to her heel. But the house had weathered many such a storm. It might bend, but it would not break. Em managed a TV dinner, finished the dishes, and went out into the living room. Her cable TV connection brought the world in on her, whether she would or no.

Between programs she stopped long enough to peer out at the house on the hill. A light sparkled from one of the windows—the kitchen, she thought. But what is he going to do about a bed? All the bedrooms were on the second floor, and there was no way he was going to get himself upstairs!

By ten o'clock, tired from her days and nights with Mrs. McCloud, Em fumbled her way up the stairs, holding on to the banister because her eyes were only half open. The storm had ended, but clouds still cloaked the stars, and high dark clouds hastened by on their way to the Atlantic Ocean.

A nightgown? She had a dozen or more. All sedate, solemn, throat-to-ankle coverage, and for some reason she wanted something different. So she turned and went across the room to Rob's closet. One of his Harvard T-shirts, meticulously washed and stored, flowed down below her knees. She clutched at its material for a moment, daydreaming, running her hands up and down the football emblem that swathed her breasts. Dear Rob.

She stooped to look out of her bedroom window. The light still sparkled from the house next door. She shook her head, not understanding her own emotions as she climbed into the king-size bed. Sheba had become too old to vault up on to the bed beside her. Instead the cat curled up on the throw rug that held pride of place in the middle of the room. Em treasured that rug. It had won a prize the year she had braided it in her high-school home-economics class. Her teacher had been proud, her friends amazed, and Gran, when she had brought it home, had said, "Hummph." A pretty big accolade from an old New England lady who knew that praise should be used sparingly. She had been thirteen then; that was the year she'd begun to have visions. Psychic, the school nurse had told her.

And so to sleep.

She came awake gradually. Sheba was whining softly, squirming around on the rug. "All right, girl," she muttered, still groggy from a deep sleep. The cat whined again. The wind outside had dropped, but the sky was still overcast. Em's sleep had been disturbing. A child was missing, only four years old. She had wandered away from home over in the lake area. After a two-day search, the police had telephoned Emily. Not that they believed in psychics, but nothing else was working. Besides, on four previous occasions Em's visions had been of some help. But now her head ached.

There was a glow in the corner of her room, slowly growing wider and larger and brighter. Sheba, nose pinned to the rug, hissed in alarm; her claws came out of their pads.

Emily had seen it all before, but was unwilling to believe. Ghosts in her house? She had mocked it for a year, judging it to be a figment of a tired mind. All a dream, she told herself. And yet . . . did she really get up out of a warm bed and move toward the figure in the glow? Or was it all her very fertile imagination? "Fey," her grandmother had called her. "Rob?"

And there he was, dressed casually in pants and sweater as he had been on that last day. But there was no damage to his face, only a smile.

"Em?" Said sibilantly, in a soft undertone. Sheba mewed. The figure waved a cautionary finger, and the animal grew silent.

"Rob. You've come again. Oh, my darling." Although she knew better, she ran toward him, and reached her hand out to touch his cheek. Her fingers passed through the plane of his face and felt nothing. It was hard to keep from crying. "Oh, Rob!"

"Are you happy, Em?"

"Happy? Without you? How could I be? I live the days one at a time, waiting for when we can be together again! And you—are you happy, Rob?"

"No, Em, darling. I'm tired of this place. I want to go on, but it's not possible."

"Why not?"

"Because I have to see that *you* are happy. You have a long life ahead of you, Em. You have to put the past behind you, and move forward. There will be other people, love. Perhaps even another man."

"No. That's not possible. I'd——"

"You cannot keep yourself locked up away from life, Em. Remember the words? Until death us do part? It's happened, Emily. It's happened."

"But I—no, don't go now! Don't!"

"I only have a little time, Em, darling. You have to make another life. The man up the hill. He needs you."

"I don't——"

"He needs you now, Em."

"But I can't, Rob. I don't have the courage! I really don't."

The figure before her began to fade. Emily Sturtevant gave a little sob. As if from a distance she heard the words, "You'll find the courage, Em. Dig deep. You'll find it." And the misty figure dissolved before her eyes and disappeared. Sheba squalled, and then squirmed over to Em and tried to squeeze under her foot. It made life believable, feeling that warmth, feeling the brush of the cat's breath on her skin.

Em dropped down on the edge of the bed. "It can't be," she muttered. "I'm dreaming it all. But five different times? And, Sheba, you know he's here. There's no such thing as ghosts. Impossible!"

Her hands wandered aimlessly up and fingered her hair. It couldn't be possible that, of all the houses and families in Taunton, hers could be the only one haunted. It had to be something to do with her tiredness, her longing, her quick perceptions, the depth of her love for Rob. Dear Rob, to die so young in a simple car accident. Probably something wrong with the steering, the police had said. He went off the road and into the river. Poor Rob, gone these last four years.

"Sheba. You saw him?"

Her cat whined at her. It was as good as a spoken confirmation. But what upset her the most in all this confusion was that Emily was not the type of woman to be haunted by a dead love. It didn't make sense.

"There's one way to prove it," she told herself as she got up, snapped on the lights, and hurriedly dressed. What had the message been? The man up the hill needs you?

"So I'll go up there," she announced, "and make a darn fool of myself again. Imagine breaking into his house at—two in the morning! Luckily he's in that wheelchair, or he'd beat up on me for sure. And if I find he *doesn't* need me then I'll know I'm dreaming too deeply. Maybe I need a vacation. A Caribbean cruise?" But what if he does need me? her conscience queried. That was something she dared not think upon—not at this moment. "Oh, Rob," she sobbed as she threw on a skirt and blouse over her T-shirt, and rushed downstairs. Her cat refused to follow.

Her London Fog raincoat was hanging by the front door. She added it to her wardrobe and was still struggling with the left sleeve as she burst out into the wet night and trudged up the hill.

There were a few wet leaves lying on his front stairs. She slipped on the first stair and almost took a tumble. Only a quick grab at the banister saved her. It wasn't exactly a prayer she muttered. His door stuck. At first she thought it was locked. Then she *did* say a prayer as she turned around, and applied the broadest part of her fundament forcefully against the sturdy oak. The door swung open.

The hall light was still on. She gently closed the door behind her and turned around. There wasn't an ounce of furniture in the hall, nor in the two rooms right and left as she sidled down toward the kitchen. There was a light in the kitchen. She could hear a raspy breathing sound. He's asleep, she told herself as she stepped around the threshold and into the kitchen. He wasn't asleep. Not by any means. He was lying on the floor with the wheelchair on top of him, one of its wheels still spinning.

"It's about damn time," Brad Colson grumbled. "Get this damn chair off of me. For crying out loud, I've been yelling for the past month!"

All her training seemed to have evaporated from Em's mind. "What are you doing there?" she asked inanely.

Brad shook his head disgustedly. He had thought better of this woman—this neighbor. But she was as flighty as the rest of them. "I like sleeping on the floor," he growled. "But I hadn't planned on using the wheel-chair for a blanket. Can you get me out of this—thing?"

She demonstrated that she could. And now that her hands were busy her mind settled down. Soft hands, Brad thought as they caressed his arms. And legs—and—— "What the hell are you doing, lady? I asked for help. I didn't want a free feel!"

"Your mind is about as dirty as your tongue," she answered. "I'm trying to see if you've broken any bones." The pain struck him then as her hands com-pressed the break in his foot. He yelled.

"Any *other* bones," she amended.

"Thanks a whole lot," he muttered. Surprisingly, she had managed to untangle him with a minimum amount of fuss. Now she squatted down beside him, and considered.

"Can you use your arms?"

"Of course. Are we going to fight it out?"

Em could not hold back the little grin that flicked at the corners of her mouth. "I'd bet you'd like that a lot," she commented. "No, I think if you can help by using your arms and shoulders I might be able to get you back into the chair."

"Without breaking my other foot?" Now why did I say that? he asked himself. Here she is, in the middle of the night, being the good Samaritan, and I'm treating her as if she were a leprosy case. Any decent man would at least thank her. Thank God I'm not a decent man, hey!

She had let his comment slip away as she got up, brought the chair out to the middle of the room, and set its brakes. And then she was down on the floor behind him, wrapping her arms around him, pressing the softness of her breasts into the immovable steel of his back. The feeling, the emotion, slapped him hard. It had been a long time since he had succumbed to tender feelings. All women are born soft, he assured himself—and hard.

"Well, you're supposed to help," she said almost in his ear. "We're trying to get you to sit up."

"If you had said something," he grated, "I *might* have helped."

"Come on," she snapped at him. "You're a grown man. I know it must hurt, but you're not a child. Stop feeling sorry for yourself!"

The last time someone had said anything like that to him had been on his eighth birthday. He remembered the tantrum he had thrown, almost as if it were yesterday. "Don't talk to me like that," he snapped. "I'm not your country bumpkin."

"I'll say you aren't," she returned. "All the bumpkins I know are kind, thoughtful people. Now lift your weight up off the floor and stop the wailing!"

She might as easily have stabbed him with a paring knife as have stabbed him in his male pride. He swallowed his words, put both hands flat on the floor, and lifted. She added her strength—considerable strength, he noted—and after a brief tussle he was back in the chair. "Look out for my damn leg," he roared at her.

"I'm looking after your damn leg," she returned. "And stop cursing at me. Moving a deadweight like you around is not too easy."

"Yeah—well." And when she's right she's right, he told himself. "Thank you."

She moved around in front of him. She was wearing a gamine grin on that plain face. "I'll bet that hurt," she said.

"A broken foot always hurts," he snapped.

"I meant the thank-you, not the foot."

Damn her lights, he shouted at himself. She's laughing at me. Teasing me. But what else can you expect from a redhead? They wait until they really get you down, and then they pour it on! And there she stands, both hands on her hips, dressed in every piece of clothing she owns, like any bag lady.

"And now that you've done your good deed, what next?" He had meant to snarl at her, but couldn't quite manage. After all, she didn't *choose* me for a neighbor, did she? So it all came out—not exactly in a jovial fashion, but at least with some tinge of friendliness.

"I don't know," she returned. "I really don't know. Whose stupid idea was it to leave you alone in this house with a broken foot?"

"My stupid idea," he snapped. "I'd rather be alone with a broken foot than be paired up with one of those vultures. And one of them my mother, would you believe that?"

"I find it hard," she said. "That you actually have a mother, I mean. You seem to be the sort of man who was carved out of granite. I don't suppose you'd reconsider and let me call somebody to take care of you?"

"Somebody will be along pretty soon. A whole bunch of somebodies. I just seemed to have gotten my times mixed up. But then, you said you were a nurse?"

"Private-duty cases only," she agreed.

"Then you're just what I need," he said. "Call the nursing registry and have them assign you to my case."

"Oh, brother."

"It doesn't appeal to you?"

"Look," she said, sighing, "it's been a long and difficult day—and night. My record hasn't been too good lately. Four losses and only one win. I wouldn't say that the pair of us are compatible, and that's important to a nurse. You can't do a patient any good until you work up a little empathy—you know?"

"Empathy I don't know. All I know is emergency. Isn't that the magic word in the medical trade?"

"You've got me there," she admitted. "Until morning, that is. Then we'll have to find you someone else to bear your burdens. What shall we do first?"

For the first time a smile touched his lips. Barely touched them, that was. "First things first? In that case, I'm hungry as—Hades."

"That's a good sign. When the patient remembers he has an appetite it's an indication that he's recovering."

"Do you say so? Can you come over here for a moment?"

"What's the matter? Something bothering you?"

"Here—in my right eye." She came closer, leaned against the chair, and squinted. The kitchen light was an overhead bare bulb, and the light was poor. She moved even closer.

"I don't see anything."

"No, of course not," he whispered in her ear. "I have more than one kind of appetite." His arms came around her, pinning her against him. The brakes on the chair squealed, but she was truly trapped. What does the nursing manual say about things like this? Keep cool. Be distant.

"And just what do you expect to gain from all this?" Cool enough? Well, it sounded all right, but, instead of being rejected, those oak arms squeezed just a tiny bit more, that brooding mouth came down on hers, and their lips touched.

"But——" she sputtered, and was lost. It had been a long time. Rob had always kissed her coolly and sweetly. Not this man. He was like fire, burning away into the heart of her. She attempted to struggle, but only for a moment, and then became rigid.

"Relax," he whispered in her ear, and before she could muster up the proper words her lips were sealed again. It seemed to go on for hours, but of course that could not really have been so. When he finally released her she remained in place for a moment, and then, with a gasp, she struggled to her feet and moved away from the chair.

"I hope that meant something to you," she stammered as she tried desperately to calm down, to slow her heart's mad beat.

"Yes, it did," he answered.

She stared at him, unable to muster a single coherent thought. He sat in his chair with his arms crossed, searching her down to her skin and soul with those strangely flecked eyes. And yet there was a disturbed look on *his* face, as if things were not going quite as he had expected.

An old clock sounded in the room next door. One of those eight-day pendulum clocks. The wind rustled at one of the windows and rattled it.

"So tell me," he said, "if you didn't hear me yelling, how did you know I needed help?"

Emily Sturtevant was all at sea. The aftereffects of that kiss gathered around her head like a little rain cloud. No matter how stupid her answer might be, she was unable to manufacture a lie. "Oh," she said, shrugging her shoulders, "my husband told me."

CHAPTER TWO

"Who told you?"

Emily, halfway across the room, looking for something to feed him, looked back over her shoulder. "Who told who what?"

"I said, who told you I needed help? And you said, my husband."

"Oh. That?"

"Yes, that. If your...*husband*——" he emphasized the word "—is down there waiting for you to come back I don't want you hanging around here. Not even for one night." His face twisted into a distorted grimace. "Get lost, lady."

Oh, Lord, Em thought. How could I get myself in such a mess? So what will I do now? Tell him that I'm a psychic? Or that I was down in my kitchen for a last glass of milk? Or that I always sleep with my bedroom windows open? Or just the simple truth, and let it go at that?

"If it makes you feel any better, he isn't—down there waiting, I mean."

"Well, he *ought* to be." And what made me make a statement like that? Bradley asked of himself. Only a nurse and she has me that much confused? And, although she's a nice kid, I've seen plenty who are prettier. On the other hand, she has *something*. Some attraction I've not been up against before. For some reason—I'd like to have her around. But not if she's already married.

26

"Thank you—I think," Emily said. "I'm not traveling under false pretenses, Mr. Colson. I've been a widow these past four years. If you want me to leave I'd be glad to see the back of you. On the other hand, if you want me to stay I could——"

"Stay," he said quickly. "Stay. You're right." A widow for four years? "Only an idiot would isolate himself out here in the woods just because of pride." But—the short hairs on the back of his neck rose—how do you equate the two statements? My husband told me you needed me. I've been a widow for four years! And do I dare ask for an explanation? Probably not—just now.

"The cupboard is pretty bare," she said as she fumbled through the cabinet above the sink. "You can have canned beans, or you can have bagels and cream cheese." After a moment she amended the statement. "Stale bagels."

"So why are you still wearing a wedding ring?"

"Do you think," she begged, "that we could keep the conversation on one subject at a time?" There was velvet in her voice, and a hidden deeper sarcasm.

"So answer my question. It was a pretty simple one."

"Simple questions require complex answers," she said softly. "Rob—my husband—was a wonderful man. I wear his ring because I've never, ever met anyone who could take his place. In fact, I don't think I'd *want* to meet anyone to take his place. Does that satisfy you?"

"I wish I had known someone like you a long time ago." His nose required blowing, or perhaps his eyes were watering, or something of the sort. He reached into his pocket for a handkerchief and turned his head away from her. Then, after a contemplative bit of staring between them, "I'll have the bagels *and* the beans."

"Both?"

"It's my *foot* that's broken, not my stomach. I'll bet you're one real hard-nosed nurse."

"You'd better believe it," she muttered as she turned away from him, looking for the can opener.

Being busy required another change. For some reason—physical exercise or mental perhaps—she was perspiring madly. Em slipped out of her raincoat and dropped it on a chair. The top three buttons of her blouse were already in disarray, but the coarse cotton of her T-shirt nightgown had a high collar. Besides, she told herself, the light is pretty poor in here.

The beans heated with a little sizzle. An occasional drop or two of rain off the eaves made a comforting thump, and when she had all the food done to a turn and loaded up a plate for him there was another noise. A slight buzzing sound, punctuated by a tiny whistle. Brad Colson was fast asleep, coiled up in the uncomfortable space of his wheelchair.

"Oh, brother," she half whispered. "Men!" For a moment she stood and glared down at him, and then the glare gradually changed to a perky little smile. Seen close up, he was not so ugly after all. Up on his feet and back in harness, he might be a very handsome man indeed!

So rather than shout at him she went exploring. In the room next door, evidently a living room, there was a large low couch. Back to the kitchen again, and out of the patience of long experience she urged the wheelchair next door and positioned it beside the couch. He stirred not a muscle as she did so. The seat of the chair was somewhat higher than the couch, not a bad thing for her next maneuver. Before she attempted to move him again she gently slid up his left pant leg and examined the soft cast. It ran from his toes up to just below his knee, and was solid enough to take some careful handling. Obviously the surgery had taken place just a short time ago—perhaps even this morning? Hospital beds were in short supply, and the new federal directives required administrators to keep the patients moving.

"Mr.——" She leaned over him, her cloud of hair settling on his face and chest. For the life of her she couldn't remember his name. Raul? Sad? Rad? No, Brad! Brad Colson. "Brad," she whispered gently, her mouth but an inch from his ear. He stirred slightly, and then went back to sleep. "Brad, I have to move you—just a few inches."

He grunted.

And now came the hard part. Urging him along, she got him up on his right foot, facing away from the couch, the weight on his left side resting on her shoulder. Another check to be sure his left leg was free, another check to make sure she didn't break one of her own ankles, and she guided him slowly backward until his weight was on the couch, his head resting on a pillow, and her head tucked indecorously under his arm. He stirred again, and then resettled himself.

Em's feet now were truly tangled in the wheels of the chair; her head was firmly fixed under his arm. There seemed to be only one way out; she relaxed all her muscles and fell onto the couch beside him, her head slipping out of its trap, but one of her feet still caught in the chair.

Her eye caught his face as his eyelashes fluttered. Em took a deep breath to settle her suddenly upset stomach. This was the difficult point. If he woke up he'd be sure to hurt himself—and maybe Em too. "It's all right," she muttered. "Just getting settled for the night. Close your eyes, Brad."

He did just what she told him. Unfortunately in the doing his big left arm came down over her shoulder, and the massive ham hand on the end of it landed on on the plump curve of her buttock and fastened there. Em's eyes flew wide open. There was a nice feeling to all this, but women of her age and position shouldn't be going in for "nice" feelings. This was something not covered in the nursing handbook.

"No," she muttered. His hand squeezed. "No," she repeated.

"Not tonight?" His voice was slurred. He was either fast asleep, or the best actor in New England.

"Not tonight?" he repeated. Or at least that was an approximation of what he said, for a tiny smile played around his lips and distorted his voice.

"Not tonight," she repeated. His muscles relaxed; Em quickly weaseled her way free, then sat for a moment on the foot of the couch, feet tucked under herself, and contemplated.

"Why, he's wearing a moustache," she whispered to herself. "A little black moustache. I wonder why I didn't notice that before. Stiff, or soft?" Her index finger outlined the sparse growth. Soft—remarkably soft. She snatched her hand away as if the finger had been burnt. I wonder what it's like to kiss a man with a moustache? she thought. I should have paid more attention when he was kissing me! Rob had abhorred moustaches. He had shaved every day, whether he'd needed to or not. Of course, Rob's hair had been stiff and coarse. What the devil are you thinking about, Emily Sturtevant?

Temptation put away—or at least behind her—she stood up beside the couch, made a pillow-platform for his head, then swung his feet up on to the couch. Brad Colson teetered for a moment, then his weight shifted and he plumped down, outstretched. Em expected an outburst; what she got was a big smile, a long stretch, and a purr of contentment as he fell back into a deep sleep again.

A successful nurse always had to have the answer to the question "And what do I do next?" Emily felt very unqualified indeed at just that moment. The old pendulum clock was striking four. Four in the morning. The clouds had begun to speed away, and there was the veriest tinge of light coming in the east windows.

Wafting its way in through the doors was the smell of those beans in tomato syrup, the toasted bagels, and just a touch of coffee. Rule number two in nursing was "Eat when you can." Em grinned, saluted her unconscious patient, and strode back into the kitchen. *His* breakfast tasted like ambrosia. She stuffed the dishes into the sink, ran hot water over them, and went back to the living room.

Across from the couch was a big overstuffed chair. Em curled up into it, kicked off her shoes, and lay down for an uncomfortable minute. Her layers of clothing were too tight. She struggled back up to her feet and stripped down to her T-shirt nightgown. The chair received her with open arms. She coiled up with her head on one of those huge arms, her eyes blinked twice, and Emily Sturtevant was gone.

The doorbell gave a halfhearted tingle. Em opened one eye and checked her watch. Eight o'clock. It must be a dream. She closed her eyes, hunched herself up tighter in her coil. The doorbell rang again. It clearly wasn't a dream, and one more blast would awaken her patient. Em struggled to her feet and made a dash for the door.

"Don't you dare ring that bell again!" she threatened. The little man in the bowler hat halted, one pointing finger not more than an inch away from the bell button.

"Ma'am?"

"Don't ma'am me, and don't ring that doorbell. Please go away. We've had a hard night and we never buy anything at the door!"

"I can see you have," the little man returned as he looked her up and down. "Had a hard night, that is."

Emily suddenly became conscious of the fact that she was wearing only a T-shirt. She stepped back into the house and half closed the door, hiding behind its panel.

"What I don't see," the little man continued, "is how he could do it. That was a pretty nasty fracture. I thought that might—perhaps—blight his...normal...reactions. Now if you would kindly let me in, ma'am, I'll get things in hand. Perhaps you might dress. After a bit I'll call you a cab."

"What in the world are you babbling about?"

The little man sighed, took off his bowler, and wiped the inside of it with a white handkerchief. "Madam should not suppose," he said delicately, "that she is the only female ever to find herself in Mr. Colson's—hands." He had been about to say "bed," and barely caught himself in time. Em, who could translate that part easily, began to turn pink.

"In general, however, the master best likes it when his...overnight guests...are up and gone by the time he comes for breakfast. So if you wouldn't mind——"

Emily had finally solved the equation. She grabbed the little man by his shirtfront and gave him a lusty shake. "Your mind must be as narrow as your shoes," she snapped. "For your information I—didn't. I happen to be a nurse, and I'm here on medical business!"

Said at her Sturtevant haughtiest.

"If madam says so," the little man said. "I'm glad Mr. Colson has finally found someone with imagination. Now——" He turned out to be a very strong little man. Emily found herself standing on the porch, clutching her T-shirt around her against the stealthy kiss of a cool north wind.

"My—coat," she protested.

"Coat. Ah, of course." The front door closed in her face, to be opened almost immediately. The little man was holding her raincoat in one hand, and some of her other unmentionables in the other.

"Your coat," he announced. "And perhaps these are also——"

"There's no need to make a scene about it," Emily barked at him. "I'm going! Tell Mr. Whatchamacallit that nothing pleased me more than the thought of leaving him. And as for you, you little—what's your name?"

"Alfred," he said, and before she could start off on the six-thousand-word diatribe that crowded her mind the front door was shut very gently but firmly in her face again.

Em stood for a moment on the porch, rehearsing what she might say should he open the door again. But it was quickly obvious that she was fighting in a losing cause. The door would probably never open again. She stumbled down the stairs into the wet grass, wondering where her shoes might be, and hobbled down the slope to home. Sheba was waiting for her inside the front door.

"I can't think which one of them is the worst," she rehearsed to her cat. She fell into a kitchen chair and began to rub her chilled feet. "Him with the broken foot, or Alfred with his broken head! I hope neither one of them can find his way down the hill!" Em knew very well that she hoped no such thing. She blushed madly and rubbed harder.

Sheba sat patiently in front of her for all of a minute, and then began to sound off. "Not you too," Em criticized. "Why do *you* have to be the only cat in Taunton who gets fed twice a day?" Wearily she came to her feet, found the cat food, and satisfied Sheba's ego. "And now go chase a dog," she informed her. "But don't come near me again today!" Sheba must have felt terrible at the reprimand. She ate and licked the plate and yawned, then curled up on her favorite chair in the living room and fell asleep.

"Damn them all," Emily told herself firmly as she went up the stairs. It was still dark in the upper corridor, what with the shutters on all the windows being closed. She made her way to the bathroom and fumbled inside for the button.

The light came on without her touching the switch. It wasn't exactly the electric light, either. Rather it was a pale circular glow. "Oh, no!" Em watched the circle of light grow and brighten. "No," she repeated. "Not in daylight! Whoever heard of a ghost working in daylight? Why am I so sensitive to such impossible affairs?" But there it was.

"Rob?"

It couldn't be Rob. This apparition was a little girl, walking toward Emily, dragging a huge stuffed bear by one foot. But as she came closer she changed. No longer a little girl, but rather a small, well-developed woman. A woman with a contorted face, who seemed to be screaming at her. "Why can't you let us go?" the phantom yelled. And behind her Rob's figure, wringing his hands, his lips moving, but no sound could be heard.

"I—don't understand," Em whispered. "Rob?"

The vision began to fade. "You'll never understand," the woman shouted as she faded away.

Emily's nerves were already shot. A long sleepless night, an unfriendly morning, and now this unfriendly apparition. "Oh, God, what are you trying to do to me?" Emily screamed. Sheba, downstairs, managed to get her head up and come racing up the stairs. Emily Sturtevant was lying on the floor, screaming and sobbing, beating on the bare floor with her fists.

"Well, thank God." Brad Colson opened one eye. His field of vision was full of Alfred. Everything was just as it ought to be. He blinked the eye and looked cautiously behind the little man.

"As you say, sir."

"She's gone?"

Alfred managed a half smile while his fingers continued setting the side table. "As you say, sir."

"Alfred, damn your heart, is that all you have to say?"

"I didn't know that more was required." The little man held a fork up to the light and sighed. "Disgraceful. This silverware hasn't been polished in aeons."

Brad pushed himself up on his elbows. "I don't give a damn about the silverware. What about the woman?"

"The woman? Handled in accordance with our standard operating procedure, sir. I was surprised."

"You were surprised? You mean you just pushed her out the door?"

"Not pushed, sir. Escorted. With every drop of gentility in my body."

"And what were you surprised about?"

"Several things. She was an—interesting little thing, but not at all up to your usual standards, sir. But—well, I *had* thought that a fractured foot might . . . put you off your feed, so to speak."

"Alfred! Is that what you think of me? I'm an old lecher?"

"Thirty-five is not exactly old," Alfred remarked. "Would bacon and eggs satisfy?"

"Bacon and—— I thought the cupboard was bare."

"It was sir. I took the liberty of buying up groceries, noting that your mother was——"

"Was not likely to think of that?"

"Well—perhaps. After all, you instructed me to tell no one of this place. And if I hadn't been rounded up by the police I would have been at the hospital early enough to avoid your parent. Something to do with a paltry speed limit. And none of the other personnel showed up?"

"Not a soul," Brad told him. "And they left me stranded out on the front porch and——" And then the lovely lady came to rescue me! "But enough of that," Brad said, sighing. "Yes, bacon and eggs will satisfy. But first I'd like to get up and clean up."

The little man looked apprehensive. "We really should have a nurse," he said.

Brad Colson shook his head and grinned. "Would you believe it, I had one, but you chased her out of the house! How stupid can one man get?"

"The young lady? She was really a nurse? It's not your fault," Alfred replied. "I—thought she was one of your regular... well, you know."

Colson grinned at him again. "Even with a broken foot, Alfred? Dear God, I believe you must have insulted her worse than I did myself."

"I believe so, sir. Even with a broken foot." The little man wrinkled his long sharp nose, and knelt down beside the couch. "Now, then, if you would kindly put one hand on my shoulder..."

The long maneuver ended, freshly shaved, Brad Colson sat at the kitchen table, having surrounded a very satısfactory breakfast. "You know, Alfred, we've been together now for how many years?"

"As best I remember, sir, eleven years. I trust that the fact I—er—evicted the young lady is not about to terminate our relationship?" As he watched Colson eat the little man was flitting around the kitchen, opening windows. And then, without waiting for an answer, "I distinctly remembered telling the lawyer that the house must be aired. Whatever caused you to pick this—place?"

"Dump, you were about to say? This once was my grandfather's house. And no, it would take more than a mere woman to disturb our—relationship, Alfred."

"Do you expect to stay long? I understand the fall season is delightful in Bermuda."

"Yes, I intend to stay," Colson said, laughing. "Maybe we'd better recruit some staff before we——"

"Expire," Alfred interrupted. "I'm glad you feel that way, sir. I had already taken steps concerning the domestic staff. But what about the corporation?"

"I've got a small team on standby from the corporation," Brad Colson said. "We're going to beat off these pirates, and send them back to their little caves." The smile disappeared. "The lot of them. I'm sick and tired of working day and night so the rest of this family can enjoy life. Maybe breaking my foot wasn't such a terrible accident after all."

The little man, having finished his round of window opening, came back to stand at Colson's side. "Breaking your foot *wasn't*—are you feeling at all well, sir? Perhaps a draught is blowing on you?"

"There's nothing blowing—what was that?"

That was a multiple sound wafting its way up the hill. The ear-piercing wail of a keening cat—followed by the screams of a woman!

"From the house at the base of the hill," Alfred reported as he leaned out of the window.

"Crazy neighborhood," Colson said, and then almost jumped from his chair. "Emily," he snapped. "Quick, Alfred, get me down there! Quickly!"

"Perhaps just *one* of the neighborhood's crazies," Alfred muttered as he started to maneuver the wheelchair out of the front door. "Every New England town has a few of them."

"I heard that," Colson snapped as he held on to the chair's arms, ready for a bumpy ride. "The bounden rights of a faithful old retainer?"

"And I'm not that old, either," the little man muttered as he guided the runaway chair down the slope.

Sheba heard them arrive, and came scuttling down the stairs and out into the front yard as if the devil himself were pursuing. "Nice cat," Alfred said cautiously. Sheba snarled and spat at him and then raced back toward the door and hesitated, looking back over her shoulder. Unlike a dog, which might wiggle and jump in excitement, the big cat sat stoically until Brad wheeled his chair up beside her.

"Emily," he told the animal. "Find Emily." The cat broke from his grip and scuttled for the front door. "There's something wrong with the girl, Alfred. Go ahead. Leave me here."

The little man nodded his head and dashed into the house after the cat. Brad sat in his wheelchair and cursed the broken foot that kept him tied to it. The accident had culminated a series of foolish little mistakes. First, he had lost his temper over a little thing. His team of lawyers, spurred by his mother in his absence, had authorized the sale of so much of the stock in his own company that he had almost lost control. And then his own mother had tracked him down to his yacht, riding in Plymouth harbor. Her interest was simple: she wanted an increase in her living allowance.

"How can you possibly spend thirty thousand a month?" he remembered asking angrily, and she had turned to her sure winner—big blatant tears.

"You might as well turn it off, Mother. The waterworks has had its last successful run."

"Oohhh," she roared in fury. "You are a terrible man. Just like your father. Worse. More like your grandfather. And I brought Eloise down to meet my son. My son! Hah! My monster. My unfeeling, monstrous child." At that point she had charged at Brad with her umbrella raised, and he had ducked. Unfortunately little Eloise, an absolute stranger to the dispute, and his mother's newest protégée, had slipped on the deck behind him and tripped him up. His foot had bent the wrong way— and here he was, immobilized in a wheelchair, worrying, for no particular reason, about that girl . . . his neighbor.

Alfred was back in a matter of minutes. "The . . . young person . . . seemed to have fainted, sir. She made some statement about—haunting. Very strange. I thought her to be an eminently practical person, but ghosts? I helped her down to her kitchen and started the water for tea. Her cat attacked me all the way down. The—er—lady seems to be physically all right. Would you care to be taken back up the hill?"

Go back up the hill? He pondered. For a man who lived by split-second decisions, that momentary delay was a giveaway, and a tiny worry curve touched the corner of Alfred's mouth.

And why shouldn't I? Brad demanded of himself. I'm free to do what I damn well please. If I feel like staying I'll stay. Or vice versa. Nobody is going to put a leash on me. But nobody!

"Help me up into the kitchen," he ordered, and immediately asked himself why he had said that.

"The kitchen," Alfred acknowledged. He slid under Colson's arm, offering leverage, and struggled to get Colson to walk up on to the veranda. "You seem to have gained a little weight," the little man panted as he managed to guide them through the door and down the hall.

"I've lost twenty pounds," Brad said pointedly. Alfred shrugged his shoulders and staggered into the kitchen.

The steam kettle was whistling as they came in. The room was smaller than his own, but then the entire house was tinier.

Emily, still flustered, struggled to her feet and smoothed down her dress.

"Good morning, Mr. . . ." His name faded completely from her mind. His name, but not his understated handsomeness.

"Brad," he interjected. "Never mind the mister. My father was the mister in our family. I'm just Brad. How are you feeling?"

Why doesn't he just come over and hold me, then he'll find out how I feel? Emily thought. What if he did push his way over and put his arms around me? What then? Her hands automatically hugged herself to stop the shaking. Why am I shivering like this? The ghost didn't affect me that much, so why now? "Can I——" she paused to take a deep breath "—make you some tea?"

He brushed her statement aside. "What happened?"

"I—you wouldn't believe."

"That's right," Alfred added. "You wouldn't believe, Mr. Colson. I'll make the tea."

"Just so somebody begins to tell me something before I lose my temper," Brad growled. He edged over to the table with Alfred's help and settled into one of the kitchen chairs. Em sank into the chair beside him, and suddenly realized she had made a mistake. The chair on the other side would have been better. Out of his reach, at least. But when she started to move his hand fell on her shoulder. She sank back.

"Well?"

"The house," she stammered. "Would you believe my house is haunted?"

"At this point I'd believe almost anything." He patted her shoulder comfortingly. Em reacted to the sympathy. Gradually, like the Leaning Tower of Pisa, she began to bend in his direction, until finally she toppled over, with her head on his shoulder. And then the tears came.

I hate weepy women, Brad reminded himself. But this one isn't like all the others. This one was slim and soft and warm—and needed him. He made comforting noises and put his arm around her. And needed him! The phrase stuck in his mind, creating an echo. Among all his crowd of relatives, all the thousands who worked at Colson Enterprises, there wasn't a soul who really needed him. Well, Alfred excepted, perhaps.

"All right, now, Emily." She sniffed a couple of times. Alfred, the perfect man's man, instantly proffered a clean handkerchief. Em used it to dry her eyes and then tried to sit up, but Brad's hand held her down.

All right, she thought, if that's what he wants—she wiggled into a better position. It would be foolish to struggle to be free when she didn't *want* to be.

"Now," he prompted.

"I—don't know where to start."

"Always start at the beginning." She squirmed around slightly so she could see his eyes. The gold flecks seemed to be spinning in circles, but of course that couldn't be. People don't have golden eyes, and certainly not ones whose pupils spin. All nonsense. I'm losing my marbles, that's what I'm doing.

"Now," he repeated.

"My house is haunted," she said firmly. "It is."

"Okay." His arm gave her a little squeeze.

"It's been haunted for four years, but now things are worse."

"More than one ghost?"

"Two." Em sighed as she wrapped both her hands around his arm. For support, of course, she told herself. Just for physical support.

"For four years, two ghosts?"

She thought that over judiciously. It wasn't true, but did she dare to tell him so? "No. The second one, a woman, appeared just this morning. Isn't that silly? Who ever heard of ghosts walking in the morning?"

"Who ever heard of ghosts walking at any time of the day?"

"Alfred, shut up. Where's that tea?"

"See," Em muttered as she warmed her chilled fingers on the hot mug. "That's why I didn't tell anybody. Who'd believe?"

"I would," he answered softly. "Did you recognize either one of these spirits?"

"Yes, Lord, yes. My—husband, Robert."

"And the woman?"

"I haven't the slightest idea."

"And Robert. What sort of husband was he?"

Em cuddled up closer to his warm arm. "The best," she answered. "The very best. I loved him, and he loved me, and——"

"He never, for example, spent a number of nights away from home?"

"Well, of course he did," she objected. "Rob was a salesman. He was on the road two weeks in every four, working for—isn't that strange? He worked for the Colson corporation.''

"Just a coincidence." Brad tightened his grip and felt the softness of her response. There was no doubt about it, this woman was all woman. "There must be a thousand Colsons in this area. But why would he come back to haunt you?"

"I don't know, do I? If I knew I'd tell you." Or would I? Was there anything about Rob's appearances that seemed out of place? Outside of that worried expression he wore? It was the same "little boy lost" look of his when he had been up to something. Never anything major, of course, because he was so loving. And the woman? Who could she have been? Or maybe they aren't together. Emily tried to shake her head, to no avail. She was trapped by Brad Colson's massive strength. Pinned against his shoulder—right where she wanted to be at this particular moment. She would explain it to Rob the next time he came.

"It's plain to me that you've been through a terrible experience," Brad told her. "So the first thing we'll do is move you, bag and baggage, up to my house. I need a nurse anyway. Drink your tea." A pause. "Now what's the matter?"

"I can't drink my tea as long as you're holding my head on your shoulder."

"Oh." The pressure was released. The tea was already cold, but she drank it anyway. It might help to control her shaking.

"Alfred, when are those other people due to arrive?"

"The domestics?"

"Yes. The domestics. Why do I find that hard to say?"

"A typical American egalitarian condition," Alfred said. There was a smirk spreading all over his face.

That's what's so strange, Em told herself. British! All over his British face!

"They have already gone up the hill," Alfred said.

"Good. You go ahead. Get some female to come down and help Emily pack, and some husky man who can push me up the hill without coming out all over with palpitations."

"Well, really," Alfred said under his breath. "I pushed you *down* without any problem."

"Well, really," Emily said under her breath. "A darn dictator, are you? Lord of the manor?" But secretly she was glad to have someone take over her floundering life, even for a minute. "Come on, Sheba," she called, "let's go see how the other half live!"

CHAPTER THREE

"So I——" Emily started to say, and then another person whizzed by between them. They were sitting in Brad's living room, she on a straight-backed chair on one side of the room, he on the couch across from her.

"I'm damn sick and tired of this wheelchair. Bloody monstrosity," he had told her. So she had spent a physical ten minutes getting him moved.

"Where are they all coming from?" Em asked. Her little nose wiggled at the perplexity of it all. Yesterday the house had been empty; today it was like Grand Central Station. Two men were working on wires on the other side of the room. Computer faces winked and blinked at her. A keyboard was just under his hand.

"Alfred's been busy, as usual." He waved a casual hand at the mob scuttling around. "You were about to say?"

"Alfred's a *very* busy person," she agreed. Caution lights hung in front of her eyes, but she went ahead into the unknown. "Has he always been around, rearranging your life?"

"Not always." His smile expanded. Teeth "big enough to eat you with" glistened at her. And when he cocked his massive head at her he looked as pleasant as a brown bear. Almost human, that was. Em took a deep breath. He did that to her. Unsettled her stomach just by being there. It wasn't entirely fair, and she resented it. The only solution to her problem was to be Nurse Sturtevant. Unconsciously she squared her shoulders for battle and reached up to straighten her cap—which, unfortunately, she had left down at the other house.

"So I called your doctor," she said all in a rush. Her cheeks spread her blush. Her hand wandered to her hair—and pulled just the wrong hairpin. That mass of golden red on top of her head collapsed and sent the soft tendrils down over her face and down her back. She brushed it aside irritably. His grin disappeared.

"Did I *tell* you to call my doctor?" The coldness of a northeaster cloaked the words. Storm warning.

"No, you didn't," she snapped. "It's one of the duties of a nurse to keep in touch with the doctor in the case, and that's what I'm doing!"

"If there's one thing I hate it's imperious women!"

"So? We should all be soft and sweet and grovel at your feet?

"Not necessarily at my feet, but grovel, yes. Is that what you think of me? A case?"

"I don't want you to think that I *ever* think of you." She fought back gallantly. "In the personal sense, that is."

His grin was back again. "You really don't like me, do you, Emily?"

"I wouldn't quite say that. I'm...indifferent to you—that's more like it. Does that make you angry? Now that you've got some help, do you want to fire me?"

"You're the only nurse in the neighborhood," he drawled. "I'd be a fool to fire you at this stage of the game." His eyes wandered up and down her slender frame, from the mass of hair she was vainly trying to bring into order, to the slim, narrow naked foot. Somehow, in all the moving, she had lost her shoes. The loss put her at a disadvantage with this man. She tried to tuck her feet up and out of his line of sight. He laughed as if it were the funniest joke since sex had been invented.

"No use squirming," he advised. "No doubt about it, you are the perfect woman. Just the right size and shape, with the most proper training—and you don't like me. Every possible advantage, and it all fell on me like a bolt out of the blue. You talked to my doctor. How is the old quack?"

Emily gasped. In her professional training a doctor was not considered to be God himself—but he did have many of the attributes of the archangel Michael, standing with sword in hand at one of the gates. "Quack?" she muttered. "He—— Isn't that strange? He asked how the old curmudgeon was. I took that to mean you."

"And?"

"And he said it was still true. When a patient who's supposed to have some sense checks himself out of the hospital against his doctor's advice anything good that happens to him is bound to be a surprise. Crutches."

"What?"

"Mr. Colson, you broke your foot a short time ago. Your doctor has just replaced that soft cast with a hard one. Your foot has a couple of pins to hold it together. You're supposed to be up on crutches, exercising, not sitting around like some mogul on his rolling throne."

"Hey," he complained. "It hurts. Besides, I *like* being a mogul."

"Crutches," she said. Her little chin stuck out at him with all the fierceness she could muster.

"I don't have any," he said, as if that were the end of the argument.

"Right here." Emily reached behind the door and produced a pair of wooden crutches. "I keep a couple of pairs in my closet at all times. Patients have a tendency to be...sensitive about crutches—not the crutches themselves, you understand, but rather the idea of crutches. Now if you will stand up we'll adjust them, and I'll give you a lesson in how to operate them.''

"The devil you will!"

"*Mr.* Colson!"

He was muttering under his breath, but he did manage to stand up by using the wheelchair as a replacement for his left leg. Emily produced one of those sunny smiles. The nursing kind that sent the message "what a good little man you are." And didn't mean it, of course. Behind them, Alfred came across the threshold and coughed.

"We have a visitor, sir."

"*We* have? I told you, no visitors, no door-to-door salesmen, no stockbrokers!"

By this time Emily had crossed the room and substituted her own shoulder for the arm of the wheelchair. She could almost hear him sigh as his weight came down on her soft shoulder. She shifted her feet to brace herself. Both the crutches were in her right hand.

"This is somewhat on the order of old business," Alfred said. "The young female person——"

"Oh, God, not Eloise?"

Alfred coughed into his gloved hand. "I believe this female is called Evelyn, sir."

"Evelyn?"

"Several weeks ago, sir. Miss Evelyn did not take kindly to her—dismissal. You'll remember she was the first lady in your 'E' cycle."

"You know I have a very poor memory," he grumbled.

"Don't sulk," Em told him. "This 'E' cycle sounds very interesting."

He glared at her and refused an answer. She shifted his weight on her shoulder, and then smiled at him. Alfred jumped into the vacuum. "From time to time Mr. Colson has the urge to date only women with some special letter beginning their name. Six weeks ago he changed from 'A'—Miss Ann. A lovely woman, with blond hair. She made a terrible mistake. And then he started with 'E.'"

"And now you're down to Emily," she sighed. "Poor man."

"Alfred, you gossip worse than a fisherman's wife. It's worth your job." The little man seemed to be totally reconciled to the threat. He shrugged his shoulders as Brad turned to Em. "Does it bother you?"

"Me? Not at all. I never use my given name at work. You may call me Nurse Sturtevant."

"Alfred. Go away." The little man smiled, made a very slight bow, and went off. In the distance loud voices prevailed, words indistinct.

"I thought I'd find quiet around here," he complained, as if it were all her fault. "Peace and quiet, that's what I need."

"Exercise," she contradicted. "That's what you need. Now, you put this crutch under your right arm——"

"It damn well doesn't fit," he interrupted. "It's too short."

"Don't curse. It's supposed to be," she answered patiently. "Short, that is. You're not supposed to put your weight on the top of the crutch. The weight goes on the muscles of your hands and arms."

"Only a fool would walk with something like this," he grumbled. "What the devil are you thinking about now?"

"Me?" Em came out of her retrospection. "I was thinking that I've surely had a worse patient than you, but I can't seem to remember his name. Shall we get on with it?"

Brad Colson mumbled something under his breath. Emily, who had selective hearing, managed not to understand a word of it. "Here we go," she said. "It takes two to——"

The door, which Alfred had closed behind him, opened and crashed back against its stop. "Brad Colson," an enraged female voice snapped, "just what are——?"

"Oh, God," he said. Both crutches were under his arms, but he was wavering. One of them slipped away from him. He made a mad grab for Em's arm. Off balance, the other crutch fell to the floor. Both hands reached for Em and held on for dear life. Em staggered under his weight and began to fall.

"Watch that leg," she yelled as they both rocked, swayed, and collapsed onto the couch.

It wasn't a bad fall, Em told herself. He had carefully moved his broken foot out of the way, and then bounced gently off the cushions. Em, but a fraction of a second behind him, landed in his lap, was caught up by both those tremendous arms, and was pressed against his chest. Her hair flew wildly, covering them both. Within the little screen of hair he chuckled, and before she could judge what next needed doing he provided a clue.

His lips, warm and pleasant and gentle, touched hers. There was a little electric shock, as if all his synapses were gathering current—for what purpose? Lethargically Em sighed. Her arms were trapped within his enveloping hug, and she didn't want to move them anyway.

Those lips broke contact, leaving her feeling bereft. She sighed again, and they were back, pressing gently but searching. His tongue seared her lips, pried her mouth open. Em managed to breathe just in time. His synapses had done a good job for him. A lightning bolt struck her tongue, reached her back, slid down her bones to her hips, and shook her stomach as it had never been shaken before.

It seemed like hours before he reduced the pressure. "Brad," she gasped.

"Don't," he responded softly. "No censures. Wait a while."

"I wasn't going to——" she whispered.

"Brad Colson, just what the hell do you think you're doing?" Evelyn stamped across the room, raging.

"I'm not doing anything," he reported. He brushed enough of Em's hair out of the way so he could peer over her shoulder into Evelyn's eyes. "I'm a poor invalid who just does what he's told these days. Nurse Sturtevant's in charge. Why don't you ask her what *she's* doing?"

"Damn coward," Emily spat in his ear.

"Tut tut. Let's have no cursing in this house."

"You, there." Evelyn tapped Em on the shoulder. "Just what the hell are you doing with my fiancé?"

"As little as possible," Emily complained as she fought free of Brad's arms and lap. "And, come to think of it, I don't like your attitude either. As the charge nurse in this case, may I suggest you go away suddenly? I can't have the man disturbed."

"Don't give me that lip," the blonde retorted.

"Nice work, Em," Brad Colson cheered. "Now if you could only——"

"Throw her out?" Em interrupted.

"Hah!" Evelyn snorted. "You and what army?"

Alfred peered around the door. "I could always get Alfred to do the dirty work," Em persisted. Alfred disappeared in a flash of light. Her opponent straightened up, towering a good four inches above Emily's head. But Em had not spent all those years applying muscle to recalcitrant patients for nothing. She stalked over to Evelyn and rested one hand on the blonde's elbow.

"Would you kindly leave?" she asked gently.

"Not a chance," Evelyn shouted, and then groaned. With one hand Em seized control of the other woman's elbow and lower arm, twisted the arm up behind Evelyn's back, and applied a little pressure.

"When I was a kid," Em said conversationally, "I used to watch wrestling on TV. Gorgeous George was my favorite. He and Argentina Rocca." A little more pressure was applied. The blonde leaned forward, screeched in combined anger and pain and, under urging, stomped out of the room, through the long hall, and out of the front door. Em watched through the ornate glass of the door until the blonde climbed into her car, then she symbolically washed her hands and went back to the living room.

"Well?" she said, posing in the doorway with arms folded across her breasts.

"Very well indeed," Brad returned. "Now if you could only help me up...?"

"I am not a barroom bouncer," Em told him. "And I don't expect to be used as one. Is that clear?"

"Very clear." He was a big man, with a big laugh, and a wild sense of humor. She could see him struggle to smother the laughter. His Adam's apple bounced up and down and he almost strangled himself.

"I'm sure Alfred could have handled the affair with much more aplomb," she commented.

"Yes, I suppose he could. You were about to help me up?"

"I was about to do no such thing." She glared at him with a look calculated to take the shine off any table-top. Silence reigned.

"She drives a Capri." Emily finally broke the silence. "A convertible, no less."

"Yes. Red. It cost a bundle."

"My God! You didn't——"

"I'm afraid I did," he replied meekly. "We all make mistakes and have to pay for them."

"That's it," Em snapped. "A womanizer, no less. Of the first degree. I'm going to pack up and go home."

"I wouldn't advise it, Nurse Sturtevant. It's almost five o'clock in the afternoon. Be dark in another hour, and you yourself admit that the house is haunted."

"It isn't haunted that much," she pointed out. "It's just my husband." And how about that, Emily? she asked herself. *Just* your husband. Wouldn't that hurt Rob something terrible? He was always so sensitive to things that seemed to be slurs. "And he loves me," she added for good measure.

"And how about that other female ghost? A bit of rivalry there?" Em brushed the suggestion away with a sweep of her hand.

"Give it some thought," he advised. "Thank you." During the conversation, almost against her will, Emily had been arranging him so that he might be helped up. Now she collected the crutches and extended one hand to help pull him up. "You can't count on ghosts," he added as he steadied himself on the crutches. "They're very wispy things." He had the grace to blush at the solecism. "Sometimes they go out of control, you know."

"I don't know any such thing," she said glumly. "And I'm surprised that you've become an expert on the subject!"

"I'm a quick study, Em. There was a book here in my grandfather's library. But ghosts are tied to the place and time where their death occurred. You'll be safe up here."

"Yeah, safe," she muttered. "A lot you know. My Rob went off the bridge into the Taunton River. And now he's haunting my house. How do you know he can't just come up the hill a few yards and walk in here?''

''Impossible,'' he said firmly. ''Now, how do you make these sticks work?''

He *was* a quick study. After five minutes of instruction and two hours of practice he had mastered the art of ''crutching it out.'' ''I'll leave you alone now,'' Em told him.

''What?''

''Don't be so darn indignant. Even nurses take time off now and again. Only a wife has to put up with a man twenty-four hours a day!''

''And you'd love to have that position?''

Em stopped and took a good long look at him. He was slightly bent, leaning on the crutches, but even with that handicap he stood a good six feet and more. A good night's sleep had left him composed, the wrinkles on his forehead smoothed and the sparkle in his eyes restored. There *were* golden flecks within them. Altogether a dangerous man to deal with. Walk softly, woman, she told herself.

''What position is that?''

''Wife,'' he said. ''You'd just love to be the wife of all those Colson millions, wouldn't you?''

''All those millions?''

''Oh, come off it. You've known from the start about the Colson millions. You husband used to work for us.''

''Millions, huh?''

''Lots of them.''

''Is there any way I could get one or two without having to take you on too?'' She had no intention of taking even fifty cents from him, but a million was a lot of bucks, and Em could just not help but sound wistful.

"No way," he said. "My warm bed and my millions. Tempted?"

"Not by a pig's knuckle," she told him solemnly. "I hate warm beds, and, as for you, I could buy a better man at Shaw's Supermarket with two tomato soup coupons."

"Well, that sounds impressive. I'm to take it you don't like me?"

"You can take it any way you like," she almost shouted at him.

"So how about, then, we don't get married? We just settle down to a little live-in affair, and after it's over I'll see you get a bauble or two for your trouble. How's that sound?"

"Another minute's worth of this, Mr. Colson, and I'm going to have to throw up. There's no place for you in my life. In my personal life, that is. Now, exercise. Walk up and down the hall. Try the stairs. Get Alfred to help out. I'm going down to my house to pick up a few clothes."

He walked behind her out to the front door. She's faking it, his intuition told him. A woman might hold out if the price were fifty thousand dollars, but millions? Never. She's making a bid to satisfy her conscience. Or maybe she's going back into one of her dark corners and consult with the ghost of her husband? Lord, what a weird woman this is. But nice, mind you. If my mother met her she'd go straight off her rocker. And that's not a bad idea, is it? I'll ask Em if she's interested in meeting my family. But when he turned to inquire a police car stole the show as it skidded to a stop in front of the house. Its siren died like the fading wail of a very big cat.

"All kinds of entertainment," Brad muttered. "I suppose after the police go away we have a dog-and-pony act."

"Don't be so sarcastic," Emily said. "They've come for me. Hi there, Sergeant Hill. I take it the little girl is still lost?"

"Still lost," the sergeant admitted. "Would you care to give it a shot, Miss Emily?"

"I—guess this might be a fine time to try," she confessed. "The whole day has been a madhouse. Something's gone wrong about once an hour. Come on in." Em turned back into the house and walked down the hall, the policeman right behind her.

"Don't mind me," Brad muttered. "After all, it's only *my* house." The pair of them paid him no attention at all. Em walked to the kitchen, found the most comfortable straight-backed chair, and sat down, resting both elbows on the tabletop. "What's going on here?"

Emily seemed to be settling back comfortably, not paying the slightest attention. Sergeant Hill, watching her anxiously, shushed Brad with a finger to his lips.

"She has to get settled," the big policeman whispered. "The little girl has been missing for forty-eight hours, and the routine methods haven't turned up a thing. So I suggested to the chief that we ask Miss Emily to give it a try."

"Oh, my God," Brad groaned. "Ouija boards and psychics? You people must be out of your minds. There's nothing to that psychics business. It's been proven time after time! Is this what the taxpayer pays for?"

"I'm sure you're right," Sergeant Hill said calmly. "The fact that Miss Emily has been right four times in the past two years is hardly important, right?" At which he turned his back on Brad and moved over beside Emily's chair.

"Ready, Miss Emily?"

"You did bring something personal of the child's?"

"Here. Her favorite doll, her mother says. The whole family is frantic."

"It couldn't be better. A Raggety Ann doll. Thank you." Em took the toy in both hands and ran her fingers up and down over the form of the doll.

"All nonsense," Brad muttered.

"Shut up," the policeman commanded.

"Hush, now," Em crooned as she treasured the little doll against her breasts. Her eyes turned dreamy, and then closed. Her back stiffened. She mumbled something under her breath, as if talking to the doll, and then smiled as she chanted a little lullaby. And then her eyes opened.

"Did it work?" Sergeant Hill seemed to be holding his breath.

"I think I need to throw up," Brad Colson said.

Em favored them with a big smile. "A map," she mused. "A big map of the town." Officer Hill rustled through his briefcase and pulled out a detailed map of the city. "This do?"

"More than enough." Em closed her eyes again, hugged the doll, and let her fingers stroke the surface of the map. "There," she finally said as her fingers came to a halt. "Somewhere in there."

"Good Lord, that's the high-rent district," the policeman said. "She can't possibly be wandering around out there."

"No. She's not wandering," Em said. "The family is split?"

"Yeah. Getting a divorce."

"The father?"

"He's living down in Florida. Big-shot auto dealer down there."

"Yeah," Em drawled. "My best feeling is that he's in one of those apartment houses out by the lakes. And he has the little girl with him. She's okay. In fact, she's happy."

"What, no street address and telephone number?" Brad interjected.

"We don't need another wise guy in town," the policeman commented.

"You're not going to take police action on a dippy little dream like that?" Brad protested.

"You'd better believe it," the sergeant said. "Oh, the doll?"

Em fondled the little figure for a moment, and handed it back reluctantly. "There's a deal of love wrapped up in that doll," she told Hill. "You know the father?"

"He's—known to us," Sergeant Hill said as he moved towards the door. Em, who had been raised in a police family, nodded grimly. *Known to us.* Police shorthand for a man with a record. The strain had been a little too much for her. She gave a great sigh of relief and laid her head down on her arms on the tabletop.

"Damn." Brad Colson came over to the table and gently caressed Emily's lovely hair. "A lot of wear and tear involved?" His voice was soft and low. A Lorelei could hardly have done better.

"An awful lot," she sighed. "There's a great deal of physical exertion required in these simple little psychic searches." She managed a couple of deep breaths and then pushed her chair back and got up. "Now what was I about to do before we were interrupted?"

"Run off. Quit. Take off," Brad reminded her. "Do you really believe in that mumbo jumbo?" He did his best to keep up with her, but the floor had been recently polished, and his crutches slipped. "Hellfire, I'm going

to fall flat on my face. Em?'' Alfred came out of the
kitchen to help him.

By the time he was straightened up Emily was almost
out of sight, walking down the hill. Brad Colson shook
his head, disgusted with himself, and watched her pert
figure disappear behind her own house. In a fit of pique
he yelled for Alfred, and crutched his way up and down
the big curved stairs four times before the little man could
be of any use to him.

Meanwhile Emily had marched smartly down the hill,
her back straight, her shoulders back, until she was out
of sight of the other house. There was a limousine parked
in her yard under the maple trees. Sheba was main-
taining a wary guard from her hiding place under the
porch. As soon as the cat saw Emily approach she came
out snarling and spitting.

''It's no use, Sheba,'' Em called. ''I've got your
number, kitty. You didn't have the nerve to squall until
you were sure you had support, did you?'' She bent one
knee to scratch the animal's soft, sensitive neck. Sheba
froze, then moved slightly so the fingers would be at the
right place, just behind her ear.

''A well-trained animal.'' The tall heavy woman was
the same one she had seen from a distance, the one who
had escorted Brad Colson up to the house. She struggled
to get out of the limousine, and walked over to where
Em was waiting.

''Yes, isn't she?'' Em patted the graying muzzle and
decided not to explain. Sheba was a typical cat. Independent, untrainable. There was no doubt that Sheba
knew a dozen or more commands; there was also no
doubt that she would pay no attention to any of them,
except when enlightened self-interest told her she had a
great deal to gain by doing so. Rob had spent three years
trying to train that cat. Em had always praised him for

his success; now, with a different perspective, she knew her husband had not been as much of an animal trainer as she had thought. But that made not the slightest difference to me, she told herself firmly. Everybody has faults. Even Rob. I love him just the same.

"My name is Colson," the woman said, and then waited. The voice was deep, almost as deep as a man's, and gravelly, as if the owner was accustomed to giving a great deal of instruction in a very loud manner. A man popped out of the driver's seat of the car and came around to them. Tall, almost as tall as the woman, but extremely slender. His nose twitched regularly, like some rabbit planning to run at the first chance.

"My nephew Ralph," Mrs. Colson made the introduction as if Ralph hardly mattered. "My traveling secretary."

"Er—Sturtevant," she returned softly. "I live here." She gestured toward the house.

"Miss Sturtevant, I would——"

"Mrs. Sturtevant," she corrected.

"Ah. Mrs. Sturtevant, I wonder if I might have a few minutes of your time?" Emily nodded as the man offered a tentative smile. Mrs. Colson was a plump woman in her sixties, with two chins and a mass of blue-white hair, cut artfully around the rim of her shoulders. Her mannish red blazer was buttoned, and having trouble restraining her stomach. Her plaid skirt fell an inch below her knees. Altogether, she looked like a superannuated goalkeeper on a field hockey team.

Em wanted very badly to know what was going on. Curiosity was her major vice. "Come into the kitchen," she offered. "I'll make us a pot of tea and I'll see if I can help you."

Ralph sighed audibly. Emily felt a considerable empathy with the man. He looked to be so frail that he engendered sympathy. And the way Mrs. Colson cracked her whip at him merely added to his problems. She walked beside him up the steps and whispered in his ear. "Scotch? Rum? Brandy?"

That last brought a tiny smile to the secretary's face. Em chalked up one more score for herself in the game of life. Fifteen minutes later they all faced each other across the square kitchen table. Sheba had circled the pair a couple of times, sniffing, and then decided to give it all up. She went over to her sleeping box and ostentatiously coiled up and went to sleep.

"The cat," Mrs. Colson inquired. "Does she bite?"

"When the occasion warrants. She also spits and scratches and—well, anything a well-behaved attack cat might do. She also has a bad temper, by the way. I wouldn't recommend you make a closer acquaintance. How's the tea?"

"Tea? Oh. Excellent. Isn't it, Ralph?"

Ralph, whose teacup was half filled with Napoleon brandy, made a toasting gesture and then hiccuped. The dowager looked across at him in disgust. "A relative," she explained, "is almost the worst kind of employee you can find. Ralph, get your notebook. Now then, Mrs. Sturtevant."

"Now then, Mrs. Colson?"

"Is it possible that you've become acquainted with my son Mr. Colson, in the next house?"

"It's hard to say. I've met him, we've talked a bit. That's about it. I don't know anything about his life except for his name, you understand."

"Just what we need, Mrs. Sturtevant. Just what we need. Is it possible, for a small fee, that you would be willing to take something up to Mr. Colson's house and——?"

"I wouldn't dare," she interrupted. "Yes, I sort of have the right of entry, but to *give* him something that he might not want to receive—no, I couldn't do that. It would take someone with a colossal nerve!"

"I understand," Mrs. Colson said soothingly. "He does have the appearance of a—bear? No, I wouldn't dream of putting you in such danger. All I'm asking is that you take a package with you—say, tomorrow?—and place it on his desk."

"He doesn't have a desk," she replied.

"His working place, then. Whatever." Silence—two minutes' worth.

"There was mention," Emily began delicately, "of some sort of—fee?"

"Fee. Yes, of course. A fee. It is basically a simple errand. My son and I are perhaps—not on the best of terms, and it's his birthday tomorrow. I wouldn't want to miss the occasion, even though we've had this little . . . spat. Surely you agree?" She put her hand into her purse and waited for Em to answer.

"Possibly. But there's a difficult part, and a dangerous part. The part about having access to the house. Otherwise you might have Ralph here carry it over—and you could pay him some piddling sum. Now, for me, I'd want—say—fifty dollars?" Mrs. Colson turned red. She coughed, and then shoved her hand back into her purse.

And that, Emily thought, ought to teach her a lesson. I've been dealing in world-class bribery these last two days. That chicken feed is no longer suitable for Emily Sturtevant. I don't intend to take a nickel of your money, Mrs. Colson, but I did wonder. How high are you willing to go?

"Perhaps we might say—er—twenty-five dollars?" She tugged at the collar of her blouse. Mrs. Colson had suddenly become very uncomfortable. So I'll help her along, Em decided.

"That might be good for carrying this thing one way." She smiled at her over the tops of her well-trimmed fingernails. "But then again there might be some trouble. I might have to make the trip two or three times, and bring it back the same number of times. What do *you* think?"

Mrs. Colson was having trouble swallowing. "Ha, ha," she laughed self-consciously. "You must have your little joke. It's only a birthday present for my son. All right, fifty dollars—payable after the deed is done."

And why not? Em asked herself. A little comfort for a loving mother. Oh, yeah? Even if the pair of them were forever separated, she could always send the gift by mail. Or maybe it weighed a ton or two. Why tease the woman any further? After all, having to live as Brad Colson's mother might be a terrible responsibility. "Yes," she said. "I don't know what I was thinking of. Of course I'd be glad to take it over to the other house. I'll be going in a few minutes. Your son has hired me to be his nurse, you know."

"Ah! Nurse!" Mrs. Colson's face cleared. "How fortunate. And, of course, as his mother, I feel much better knowing that he's in good hands." She turned to Ralph, who seemed to be sitting in a daze, working on his third cup of "tea." "The present," she snapped.

Her nephew fumbled at the catch of the briefcase to no avail. "Oh, never mind," Mrs. Colson snapped as she relieved him of the briefcase and opened it. The object she placed on the desk was a lovely double pen holder cast in the shape of a ship, out of semi-transparent plastic. The two pens in the holder were solid black, making an excellent contrast with the base.

"Why, that's lovely," Em heard herself say. Mrs. Colson seemed to expand—without breaking any buttons. Em picked up the piece and looked it over. "Absolutely beautiful."

"Gently," Mrs. Colson pleaded. "It is breakable, you understand."

Yes, breakable, Em told herself. Lovely, useful, and breakable. And, if I were to tell Brad Colson that they want to pay me to put the little delight in his office, would that make him suspicious? It makes *me* suspicious, but then I'm not a great business tycoon.

"Delightful," she repeated. "Lovely. I'm sure Mr. Colson would be pleased to receive it and acknowledge it. I can't tell him it's a gift from someone?"

"No, no. Mustn't do that." Em looked around. Even Ralph, happily drawing outlines with a wet finger on the shining tabletop, looked up, concerned.

"Well, all right. I'd be glad to do it. And how will you know when he sees and uses it?"

"Not to worry." Her visitor was beginning to look more and more like a jovial Santa Claus, four months early for her Christmas rounds. "We have other means of keeping track."

"If that's all, Mrs. Colson? I have a considerable amount of work to do down here before I go back up to your son's house."

It had been a bright sunny day so far; now the skies must have darkened. At least the kitchen turned darker. Sheba, who had been lying under the table with her nose resting on Em's feet, mewed anxiously. As it grew darker the cat moved to the other side of her chair. Em felt a nervous reaction. She shivered as if a cold finger had slid down her spine. "Rob?" she asked tentatively.

Both of her visitors looked at her curiously. In the far corner a ball of light was forming, and from within it Rob appeared. Just as he had looked the day he'd gone away. Em remembered every minute of it. He'd been planning a four-day sales trip out in the Berkshires. And now, even as then, he was dressed in white shirt and tie, sports coat, pants, and tennis shoes.

She hadn't noticed the tennis shoes before, because the Colson corporation required meticulous dress from their representatives. Why in the world would he wear tennis shoes? It bothered her for just a half second, and then she had something more to think about.

"Em," the apparition called. As always, his voice was hollow.

"Yes, Rob, I'm listening."

"Don't listen to this woman. She's evil."

Another puncture in her skein of beliefs. Always previously she had thought Robert to be perfect. And here he didn't even understand that she was well aware of what was going on! "I know, Rob. I know. It'll be all right. Are you well, Rob?"

"As well as I can be," the ghost said. "Until I can earn release from——" And at that moment, just as in some TV serials, his voice faded away and the light dimmed. Sheba mewed a time or two, and raced up the stairs. Emily felt the little shock that always accompanied Rob's passage. The two people at her table were staring at her.

"You heard him too?" For years she had been looking for corroboration of her story. Here was the time.

"Heard who?" Mrs. Colson asked cautiously. "All I heard was you, evidently trying to talk to something over in the corner there."

"And you saw nothing?"

"Nothing."

"Nor heard anything?"

"Nothing." Even Ralph, who evidently couldn't handle Napoleon brandy, gave her a cheerful nod of agreement.

The moment passed. Emily Sturtevant was not one to bear heavily on a subject not recognized by others. Rob had come. Rob had spoken to her. It hardly mattered that these two could not have heard.

"I—my house is haunted," she said, as if that were the complete explanation of the affair.

"How interesting," Mrs. Colson said, her tone denying her words. "Now you won't forget to take this up to the other house?"

"No, I won't forget." Em was tired. All of these meetings with Rob left her without strength. She watched as the pair got up and walked out of the room. She even heard them as they went carefully down the creaky outer stairs.

"I can't believe it, but it must be true," Mrs. Colson was gabbling at her secretary. "A witch. No doubt about it. Did you see that cat? Every witch has a familiar! A real zany. Just the sort of person we need to keep Brad confused. Why is it, Ralph, that you look swizzled? That tea was as weak as dishwater. Have you been sneaking a flask out with you again?"

"Not me," Ralph declared. It was the first time Emily had ever heard him speak. "She's a nice girl."

"How would you know?" Mrs. Colson muttered. "I don't know why my sister didn't divorce her husband before you were born."

Back in the kitchen Em laid her head down on the table and said, "It's been a tough day all around, hasn't it, Mrs. Colson?" The sound of doors slamming was all the response she could get. She had laid her electronic pager on the table by the stairs, an essential part of her nursing equipment. As she went up, the pen set in her hand, the pager squawked and static filled the air as it blocked the pager's receiver. Em grinned and patted the pen set. "Powerful little devil, aren't you?" She chuckled all the way up to her bedroom. "A bug in time saves nine?"

CHAPTER FOUR

"So, TELL me about this manifestation," Brad Colson said. The pair of them were sitting in the living room, sharing a late cup of coffee. It was two days after Em's apparition; two days after she had packed up bag and baggage and moved up the hill into his house. All the clutter of machinery was covered; a few lamps glowed at the several working positions which had been established. The workers themselves had vanished. Everything was country quiet.

"It wasn't much," Emily told him. "I was in the kitchen talking to——" The name almost slipped out. For some reason she didn't want Brad to know she had been consorting with his mother "—to a visitor, and things went sort of dark, you know, and this apparition appeared in the corner. It looked like—like Rob. He seemed to have an urgent message for me."

"What was it?"

"He told me not to trust the woman I was talking to."

"Nothing wrong with that kind of advice," Brad responded.

"Now that's the problem," Em said. "I had already decided that I couldn't trust this person. I made up my mind within the first ten seconds. So there was no need for Rob to warn me, you see. For all these years I've supposed that Rob was perfect. That he'd know things long before I would. It shook me a little to think that wasn't quite true."

"Can't even trust a ghost?" he quipped. But Em was too wound up to stop.

"And something more. He always appears in the same clothes he wore at the accident. Only—funny. He was off to an important selling trip out west, but he was wearing his tennis shoes. Can you imagine that?"

"A Colson salesman wearing tennis shoes? When we own two factories that make dress shoes? I doubt that very much. Where the devil did I leave my pipe?"

"I threw it out," she replied. "Smoking is bad for your health." The humorous smile he had been sporting all evening disappeared.

"Listen here, Nurse. Throwing out my pipe is also bad for *your* health. Just where did you throw it out to?"

Em got up from her chair and moved a few feet away, just in case. "In the garbage," she stated. "And the truck came an hour ago to pick it all up."

"God a'mighty!" he bellowed, and then sat back in his chair and struggled to regain his control. It took some doing.

"Count to a hundred," she suggested, and was rewarded with as fierce a glare as a man could offer. I'm not afraid of him, Em told herself. He's only a man, for goodness' sakes, not some emperor. And a thoroughly objectionable man at that. Why am I drawn to him? I'm really not afraid of him. Am I? The question measured her own doubts; she was surprised when he gradually calmed down and smiled at her.

"What you need to do is to find an exorcist, Emily."

"A what?"

"A priest who chases ghosts out of houses. You must know a convenient priest?"

"I doubt it," she said soberly. "I'm a Catholic myself, but I never heard of—what you said there. What is it he would do? Some sort of ceremony that would banish all ghosts in my house?" She squirmed uneasily at the thought. "You know, I'm not sure I'd want to chase Rob out of the house. It was *his* house, after all. And he must have some interest in it because he keeps coming back."

"Doesn't that strike you as strange? That he would want to come back? If we are to believe Christian doctrine, he's already in a better place than this."

"I don't know," Em sighed. "I wasn't much of a Bible scholar when I was young, and I certainly know less now than I did then. But I just have the feeling—women's intuition, I suppose—that something's wrong. And don't you dare laugh."

"Me, laugh? I'm not that sort of man. What is this feeling you have?" Since that was just the sort of man she thought he really was, she felt a little restless about telling him anything more. But then, she had no one else to talk to, and he was a...most attractive listener.

"I just have the feeling that he can't get loose from earth; that something's binding him here."

"Maybe you see too many movies," he chuckled. "Or maybe you're too sensitive to life. That's what all this psychic business is about, I think. Or maybe—if you want to talk about this you'll have to come over here." He gestured toward the empty half of the couch.

Oh, no, Emily thought. Come into my parlor, said the spider to the fly? Even with a broken foot he seems to be very—sensual? And yet...? It's been four years since—— The dim light of the lamp is good to him. It erases all the little wrinkles and scars, and gives his face a sort of pleasantness that you wouldn't believe. Why hasn't he married? Look at all he's got going for him. Given a chance, I'd—no, I wouldn't, either. It wouldn't be fair to Rob!

"There," he said as he put one arm around her shoulders. Startled, Emily almost jumped up again. In all the time she had been conducting her self-examination her feet had carried her over to the couch and delivered her into his hands. Into his warm, comforting hands.

"Now," the arm drew her closer, until her thigh touched his, "let's suppose, just for the hell of it, that Rob's appearances are real. How about this visitor of yours—did *she* see the ghost?"

It wouldn't help to lie. She had been lying to people ever since that first appearance three years ago. When she told her friends it was always with a giggle, a mocking glance. Say what you would about Brad's character faults, he was a man loaded with common sense. Maybe he could help her reason it all out. And it's comforting to sit in the warmth with his big arm to protect me!

"No, they didn't see—and they didn't hear, either. I can't recall that anyone else has ever seen my ghost. Well, except Sheba, of course. She notices every time."

"Not very convincing evidence," he said. "I know there are hundreds of people who believe in haunting and ghosts. And there are all sorts of societies to consider apparitions or séances and such. It's a phenomenon almost as famous as UFOs. But ghosts are different. I understand that there are more than three dozen castles or manor houses in Britain that are allegedly haunted. But when you lay out a real test, as Harry Houdini did, the return of disembodied spirits seems to fail."

"Harry who?"

"Houdini. One of the great stage magicians of our time. He strongly believed in ghosts and fantasy and apparitions. In fact he believed so strongly that he made an arrangement with his wife and some friends to join them on the anniversary of his death. All these people gathered around for a séance, and they heard——"

"Voices?" she interrupted. "He spoke to them, or something?"

"They heard nothing," he said. "They saw nothing."

"But that doesn't mean he won't contact them some day soon."

"His wife kept her vigil every year until she, too, died. Her friends still watch. No, I think that Houdini's evidence is pretty conclusive."

"That doesn't mean I can't believe in ghosts myself," she said with some heat. "After all, he is——"

"Was," Brad interrupted.

"Damn you," she muttered under her breath. "He *was* my husband. We had a wonderful marriage."

"Did you, now? Did you really?" She shivered. He meant something, but she was just not sure what it was. And, in the meantime, "Did you really?" His arm tightened around her shoulders. She moved an inch or two more in his direction until her head was firmly on his shoulder. It wasn't the warmth that held her, but rather an undefined feeling of comfort and security. When he tilted her chin up with his big index finger she was prepared for the kiss that followed. Ready and yearning for the contact, the emotion, the glorious satisfaction. Funny, Rob had kissed her very competently—but never as well as this.

She was still bemused as she went to her lonely bed. But not so much so as to be careless with the pen set that Mrs. Colson had given her. Only, instead of putting it carefully in the middle of Brad's workroom, she tucked it down into one of her spare shoes and stored the bundle away in the bottom of her closet.

Emily overslept the next morning. She had tossed and turned and dreamed, to no avail. Not because of ghosts; there hadn't been any. Rather she was trying to rationalize her feelings about Brad Colson. But, when she came down about eleven o'clock, Alfred was the only person in the kitchen.

"Good morning," she offered.

He looked up from his paper and managed a tiny smile. "Madam."

There was an electric coffee pot on the table. She snatched a mug and filled it up. "I need this the way I need a transfusion."

"A typical American reaction," he said, but from behind the shelter of his newspaper.

"Alfred!" she snapped.

His paper came down about halfway. "Ma'am?"

"Pay me some attention. Why is it that Mr. Colson is—hiding out in this small corner of the world? Colson Enterprises is the biggest—well, I don't know what to call it—the biggest enterprise in Massachusetts?"

"Just so," the little man replied. He folded up his copy of the *Globe* in a very precise manner, taking care that every one of the original folds was replicated. And then he laid it down on the corner of the table.

"It's a serious problem, ma'am." He paused to reflect, gazing out of the window beside him. "When the elder Mr. Colson died the business was going to—er—the dogs, I believe they say." Emily nodded encouragement.

"The old man's will left stock to a variety of people, a few shares here, a few shares there. But young Mr. Colson and his mother each inherited forty per cent. Neither of them has full control over the business, as you would note." He stopped a moment to clear his throat.

"But perhaps you would also have noticed that young Mr. Colson is—what do you call it—a go-getter?"

"Just so," Emily said. A little giggle was toying at the corners of her mouth. Alfred, with a suspicious look on his face, thought for a moment and then relaxed.

"Madam ventures to tease. Ah, well, the problems we Britons abroad have to put up with—now, as I said, the young Mr. Colson is a go-getter. As a result, most of the other shareholders are usually eager to have him lead the company."

"Usually?"

"Yes, ma'am. At the present moment there is someone who is interested in taking control and selling off certain of the company's very profitable subsidiaries. Among the supporters of the sale is Mrs. Colson, the corporation's vice president and treasurer."

"But—I still don't understand, Alfred. If he's all that efficient, and has the support of other stockholders, what's the problem?"

"His mother has called a meeting of the board," Alfred continued. "To effect at least some of the sales before this raider gets his finger in the pie—er—so to speak. But Mr. Colson is, unfortunately, suffering an illness, and is thus unable to attend any meetings. No business can be conducted for the moment. And in the interim young Bradley is telephoning additional stockholders, looking for their proxy, building up support against his mother."

"How Machiavellian," Em said, sighing.

"Who?" So Alfred's education was not really complete, Em told herself, laughing. Well, nobody's perfect! I'm glad to find he has a weakness.

"Nobody important," she said quickly. "He's a baseball player. He plays for the New York Yankees, I believe. You said his mother? Is she an officer of the corporation?"

"Yes. A most discontented one. An inside trouble-maker is always the most troublesome, you know."

No, I don't know, Em thought. I hardly understand half the words. But if I want to—be with Brad I'll have to learn. I have to know Brad and his heart and the world he lives in. Is it worth it? This is a turning point, Emily. Throw the dice. If they come up "snake eyes" you can always say, "Well, I tried," and go back to your bedpans.

"Tell me more about corporate life, please, Alfred."

Alfred was a typical man. He liked to talk, especially with a delightfully interested young lady in front of him who wanted to listen. But, even at that, he spoke cautiously. This one, he knew, would require marriage. And there was nothing so awkward as a household triangle. We've been an interesting pair, Alfred thought. Marriage to a woman like this one would certainly disturb the happy tenor of our ways.

So he kept his fingers crossed as he started to explain all the world of business. Brad Colson thumped into the room about an hour later.

"Back-room conference?" Brad asked. "Secrets from the boss? Palace revolution? These damn crutches are just not going to make it, Em."

Alfred got up from his chair, and, as if he were a mind reader, produced a mug of black coffee. He set it down at the table and pulled out a chair. Brad Colson collapsed into it as if he were tired. "Sixteen times around the house on the outside," he boasted. "There's got to be a better way."

"Crazy," Emily muttered. "Not outside the house. That's all up hill and down dale. You start to learn by using a flat surface. Let me see those sticks." He handed her the crutches and inhaled the coffee. Alfred immediately refilled the mug.

"Well, no wonder." She held the crutches up in front of his eyes. They were not exactly paired. "Some devil has lengthened this one. Who in God's green world would do a stupid thing like that?"

"Stupid, huh?"

"Very. Alfred?"

The little man who had been bending her ear for more than an hour had now executed a very plausible vanishing act. "Where the devil did he go?"

"You'll get no information from me," Brad said. He was trying very hard to maintain an appearance of innocence, and not doing very well with it. "I never squeal on a partner in crime. You can take me in, but I ain't talking."

"I don't understand you," Emily stated. "How in the world can you be an important executive in the business world, and yet be so stupid as this?"

"I know it's a puzzle." Her fist pounded the table; he rested one of his big hands over the fist and brought it to a stop. "You have to remember, Em, that I inherited the business. The stupidity comes naturally. What am I doing wrong?"

"Just about everything," she sputtered. "Look now. Follow me closely. You do not put the crutch into your armpit. You hold your weight up by your hands and arms. If your body weight rests on the rubber pad on the crutch you will eventually shut off all the blood circulating through that arm. Got it?"

"I think I've got it."

Emily Sturtevant bent her head over the crutch and began readjusting its length. Brad watched the top of her head as she worked. He was driven by a strange desire. Unable to hold back, he reached over and ran a finger through her hair. She stopped instantly, and remained motionless for a moment. Then, without looking up, she went on with her work.

He stopped when she did. Now his finger began to wander through the mass of her silky soft hair. "Like spun bronze," he said softly. He bent over and inhaled deeply. "As fresh as a baby's bath."

"Baby shampoo," she said firmly. "It's cheap." She almost hit his nose with the top of her head as she straightened up. "What kind of game are we playing today?"

"Game? I'm being perfectly serious," he replied.

"I know you are, but at what?"

The pleasant smile vanished from his face. "If I knew that, believe me, you'd be the first to know, Emily Sturtevant."

Emily stood on the front porch at two that afternoon. Behind her, the house hummed with activity, none of which required her. She had been the center of everything only twenty-four hours ago, and now she was on the outside looking in.

Alfred, it turned out, was not only a valet, but also chief cook and bottle washer. An elderly woman who followed him around was his chief assistant and mop person. A tall thin man who seemed to hide whenever Em came by was the chauffeur-handyman. The half dozen "bright young men" were actually four men and two women, who bustled around the house with vacant expressions on their faces, hands full of computer tapes, and pencils tucked behind their ears. And Emily Sturtevant had become the "gofer," a position she could not admire.

"That's your position," Brad had insisted during their noon-time argument. "When I want something, you *go fer* it!"

"In that case, where the devil have you hidden your pills?" she demanded.

"I don't need any pills!"

"Everybody with a broken foot needs a pill for pain," she insisted. "At least in the first few days. I suppose you're trying to prove you're a stoic?"

"Look, lady." He was back in his wheelchair. Now he whirled it around and glared at her. "I'm just following the doctor's orders. He said that pills and alcohol don't mix. I'm *not* taking the pill so I *can* take the alcohol. Got it?"

She hadn't "gotten" it. But now, alone on the porch to think it all over, she "got" it. He was a man who had an aversion to medicine, and therefore to medical people. He liked to hide from others—*some* others. He was engaged in some sort of machinations against his mother. Well, at least he hid in his study hour after hour and made telephone calls that were going to ensure the American Telephone and Telegraph Company had profits well into the next millennium. He used people when he felt like it, and when he didn't need them he discarded them. As with yours truly, she told herself.

She had served many a tough patient, and had left when her usefulness was questioned. But for some reason the idea of leaving Brad hurt. Of course, if she went down the hill to her own house, that wasn't exactly deserting the ship, was it? You *have* to go, she told herself, before he tramples all over you. And with that she squared her shoulders and went up to the room that was temporarily hers.

It took but a moment to fill her traveling bag. And not until she got to the bottom of the pile did she recall the little glassite pen set. "And don't forget his . . . gift," she told herself.

Moments later she banged down the stairs. Her bag was heavier than she remembered, especially since it had to be handled one-handed. Alfred was standing at the foot of the stairs. She speared him with a glare. "Where is he, little man?"

"He?"

"Mr. Colson, the light of your life." Why didn't I think of that? she asked herself. Alfred has been trying to ease me out of here since day one. It was some sort of master-servant bond that tied them together, and Alfred must be afraid I might break it.

"Oh, that person," Alfred said. "He's in his—er—study, madam. He is not to be disturbed."

"The hell you say," she snapped, and was suddenly embarrassed. He's even got *me* talking like that! She would change the words, but not the thought.

"That's what you think," she substituted. "I intend to see him."

"Madam, I'm afraid I shall have to stop you."

"You really think so?" Her sarcasm went over his head. She handed him her heavy bag, and from long habit he took it. Em hated what had to come next. Alfred was really a nice little man, but when need drove...

"And now hold this." She passed him the little pen set. He juggled the gift for a moment, almost dropping it. "And now——" Alfred stared at her in surprise. But he was not as surprised at what she meant to do as she was that she was doing it. She squeezed her right fist up into a tiny ball and slammed it into his solar plexus with all her strength.

The little man ran out of breath in a hurry, and collapsed slowly onto the floor, still holding the pen set in one hand, gasping for air like a fish out of water. Em, her tensions mightily relieved, snatched the little gift from his hand and treasured it.

"See," she muttered, "my mother didn't just teach me knitting." And with that she opened the door and walked in.

"And what the hell do you want?" Brad Colson snarled. He was still in his wheelchair, holding the phone in one hand. "Damn. You made me forget the number I was dialing. What's the trouble? Did I forget some other pills?" There was a pint bottle of bourbon on top of his desk—sipping sour mash, the best money could buy.

"No," she said emphatically. "I forgot something. This is a gift, given to me for you by a friend of yours." She handed over the little set and then hid both her hands behind her back.

"How nice. Do I get to know the donor?"

"She said she was your mother, and that she was a great admirer of yours, and hated the idea that you and she were split up, especially since it's your birthday." Pause to catch her breath. "It's a very nice little gift. I almost forgot it."

"My God, woman. You think that my mother is a *friend* of mine? What kind of a mind do you have? She hates me like mad, lady!"

"How would I know?" she asked. "Most people love their mothers. Besides, she certainly acts and thinks the way you do. I figured that birds of a feather——"

"Lady, you sure know how to hurt a guy, don't you?" He was shaking his head as he set the pen set down on the desk. "My mother, hey? A friend of mine, and she wanted to give me a gift? Why do you suppose she didn't bring it up to the house herself?"

"I'm no detective, I'm just the nurse around here. If I had a son I would expect him to love me, just because—— Oh, Lord, you'd never understand, would you? And I didn't even get the opening statement right. I *was* the nurse around here.''

The words went over his head. He was studying the pen set, twisting it around to see all the angles. ''I think we can presume that she was up to no good,'' he said softly. ''Especially since my birthday is three weeks away. So there's something related to—— What do you mean, you *were* the nurse around here?''

''Nothing at all that concerns you, Mr. Colson,'' she said. She tended him a very slight but formal dip of her head. ''Goodbye.''

''Goodbye? Hey, what the hell's going on in here?''

''Nothing,'' she repeated. ''I'm a nurse, not a darn *gofer*. I'm going *out* of here.'' She turned around and made for the door, emphasizing her anger by a flip that sent her long hair swirling around her head.

''You! Come back here,'' he roared. She was already out in the hall, looking down at Alfred. The little man was breathing better, but was not yet ready to get up. In fact, he squirmed an inch or two further away from her when she stopped.

''Alfred,'' Colson yelled from inside the room. ''Stop this crazy woman!''

''Not even if I were able,'' the little man groaned. Em snatched up her case and stalked out of the door.

''Alfred? Are you out there, Alfred?'' Brad Colson clumsily swung his wheelchair around toward the door. The crutches fell with a ferocious clatter. *Her* crutches, he told himself, not mine. He leaned over and picked one up, rubbing his big hand up and down along the shaft. The wood was fine-grained, closely finished, smooth. And above everything else it seemed to have that little tingle that *she* left wherever she went.

''Alfred?''

"Coming, sir." The little man appeared in the doorway, tugging at his shirt, brushing back his handful of hair, and speaking just a little weakly.

"You have some problem, Alfred?"

"No longer," the little man responded. His hand rubbed gently across his solar plexus, where the sting of the sudden blow still pained him. "You wanted something?"

Brad studied him for a moment or two, swiveled around to the desk and put a dollop of bourbon in his glass—and then, after a quick look at his companion, an equally large dollop in the second glass. His gesture brought Alfred across the room. The pair of them picked up their glasses in a silent toast.

"I think, my friend, that I've just made one of the major mistakes of my life," Brad said. The smooth bourbon soothed his throat as it went down. His nervous hands spun the mug back and forth gently.

"I might have also."

"You mean just recently?"

"Not more than ten minutes ago, sir." Alfred tipped up his glass and drained it. "I underestimated Nurse Sturtevant. I actually tried to—er—detain her."

"And?"

"She illustrated the old adage, 'When a skillful small person meets a skilful big person, mayhem results.' She set me down on my—er—posterior with great dispatch."

Brad studied the bottom of his glass, then gestured for a refill. Alfred did the deed, and their toast was renewed. "Funny, both of us having the same trouble with the same woman. I underestimated our Miss Emily myself." The two glasses were raised again.

"And what I don't understand," Brad continued, "is why it seems so important at the moment." He could feel the warmth of the bourbon interfering with his normal good sense. "After all, she's only 'a rag and a bone and a hank of hair'."

"Kipling," Alfred interrupted. "Lovely long hair. And somewhat more than just a rag and a bone to go with it."

"Yeah," Brad replied. "Lovely. I'd love to wake up and find that on the pillow next to me."

"Don't say that, sir." Alfred seemed to have had more spirit than his glass indicated. He hiccuped, and then managed a small sob of despair. "You go hankering after *that* hank of hair and you'd have to marry her."

Brad Colson was perhaps feeling not a great deal of pain himself as he looked up owlishly at his man. "Do you say so? The marrying type?"

"I know." Alfred grinned and tapped the side of his nose with his forefinger. "Met one of them myself, I did. Damn me if I didn't. Took me two years to get loose of her. No, don't try *that* direction."

"I don't know," Brad said, suddenly sober. "Nice hair. Lovely bowsprit. Delightful legs. Worth marrying, that one, if only she weren't so damn smart! I hate a woman who's smarter than me, and that's a fact!"

His companion fumbled with a chair and fell back into it. "Don't curse so much," he lectured, and collapsed onto the desk.

"All alone again," Brad muttered as he leaned back in his chair. "Lovely lady. Why am I so liquored up at this time of day? Why did I let her get away? What the hell—what the devil can I do to entice her to come back? Ghosts? There's something very wrong in this ghost of hers."

He was quickly throwing off the effects of the bourbon. There was something at stake here more important than almost anything. Ghosts? Just suppose it's all true. That there are haunts with messages? What is it that's wrong with Emily's ghost? Or, to be truthful, what was wrong with Emily's husband, that he was still hanging around the old homestead four years after they'd buried him? Four years. And now Brad was like a true ferret with his nose to a scent, and because of his own wide background he knew where to begin. He reached for the telephone directory and began calling.

Sergeant Howard, formerly of the Taunton police department, had been retired for two years, and time was hanging heavily on his hands. When the police car came by the house to pick him up he was glad of the interruption. He hated gardening, and only did it because his wife loved to *see* him gardening. He walked around to the front of the house.

"Yeah," he said to the sergeant driver. "I remember that case. The Sturtevant brangle. Daughter of Captain Sullivan, she was. A fine upstanding man, the captain. Taught me all I needed to know with one hand tied behind his back. Sure, now, some lad wants to talk about the case? I'd be happy to come along. Only go quietly. Harriet still thinks I'm weeding that damn broccoli!"

Hardly ten minutes later he was deposited in front of the big house on Briggs Street, and invited in to the neighborhood of a bottle filled with Irish Cream, which, as every Hibernian knew, was the world's finest.

"And so you're old Danny Colson's boy? No meaner man ever walked the face of the earth. Grew up together, we did, down at the Weir. Knew your father well, man and boy. Just the man we needed to go on the cops, but he claimed he could steal more money on Wall Street. And he did, didn't he?"

Brad Colson topped off the retired police officer's glass, and tried to steer him back to the right channel.

"The Sturtevant case? Yes, that was during my time. Very nasty operation, that. Had to hush it up, you know.

Word straight from the chief. Didn't want the widow to know. We all thought a lot of Miss Emily. Well, the facts as I remember them are like this. It was a dark foggy night, and Sturtevant—yes, Rob Sturtevant—was driving that heavy car of his down through the Weir area at maybe seventy-five miles an hour, and couldn't make the turn. Car went flyin'' off the road and fell into the river. Couldn't nothin' be done, you know, that late at night. It took forever for the rescue crew to get there, and by that time—well, you know how it goes. Drowned.''

"Alcohol?"

"Well, I gather he must have hoisted a few. They did a blood test during the autopsy. He was way over the legal limit. I mean by a whole bunch."

"Drunks aren't exactly something new in Bristol county," Brad challenged. "Out of all the driving-while-intoxicated cases in town, how come you remember this particular one?"

"Oh, no. Drunks aren't exactly new in Bristol county. No reason at all to remember an ordinary DWI. But this one was hushed up. The problem was that there was two of them in the car, both dead. The girl was nineteen years old and pregnant."

"Nineteen and pregnant," Brad mused. "And the widow never knew?"

"Nope. Would have broke her heart. The chief himself put the lid on it and the mayor agreed."

"Political influence?"

The old man's expression became guarded. Brad was no longer looking at a red-faced beat cop, but rather a man who had learned something from life. "Not political influence the way you mean it," he said. "There's a difference between justice and law. We all chose justice, for the widow's sake." He hoisted himself ponderously to his feet and shook his head. "Thirty-two years on the beat," he sighed. "My feet'll never recover. Well, always glad to help. Come around some time; me and the missis have been sitting at home for two years, tryin" to grow the finest broccoli in the county. You ought to come and see it, take some home with you."

"Who, me? I hate broccoli."

"Me too." He shook his grizzled gray head. "But my Harriet, she thinks it's wonderful. Me, I'd rather have two tickets to Fenway Park, but..."

And that, Brad Colson told himself as he made a contribution to the Policeman's Benevolent Fund, is one end of this very large ball of string. Now all I have to do is unravel the entire thing, and I'll have a story worth telling. "Because," he told himself as his fingers drummed on the table, "there's no possibility that you'll catch Emily Sturtevant without first getting her to forget her first husband."

He stopped for a moment to pour himself another shot of bourbon, only to have her accusations ringing in his ears. No doubt about it, he thought. Pills and bourbon don't mix. So suppose we try pills and Emily. Slowly, half resisting, he pushed the drink away.

Tennis shoes, huh? Not in the Colson company. Now if I can only get my hands on a few more facts maybe I'll be able to convince her that her husband was not exactly the plaster saint she thought him to be. That's the way to exorcise a few ghosts. Hell of a thing for a neighborhood, having ghosts in the area! Nothing good could possibly come of it!

Chuckling to himself, he reached for the bourbon, then pushed it away again, picking up the bottle of painkillers and shaking out his ration for the day. "Here's to crime," he toasted. The taste of the water used to chase the pills down was so strange that he almost choked himself.

CHAPTER FIVE

EMILY STURTEVANT was tired when she came back home from her private-nursing case. A week earlier she had walked out on Brad Colson, meaning it to be a warning to him. A warning that he could not play with her hand and heart. He had never called her back. That seemed to be a very definite message.

When she checked in with the nursing registry there were three prospective patients waiting. Emily took the first one, little Bobby Moore, who had fallen off his second-floor balcony and only managed to collect a dozen or more scratches and cuts, and a green-stick fracture of his left arm.

Bobby's mother had screamed when she'd seen her son falling, and had run down the two flights of steps at full speed. At the bottom she'd tripped over Mrs. Mergatroyd's cat. A broken leg, a dislocated shoulder, and a concussion, the doctor had said. For Bobby's mother, not the cat. It had made for an interesting pair of cases.

When no longer needed, Em came back home, dead tired. The season had shifted further into lively autumn. She drove up Briggs Street with the sunset in her eyes. The tang of burning wood touched her nostrils. She inhaled deeply, and smiled.

It was too dark to see the brilliance of the leaves, but she could see some bare limbs silhouetted against the evening sky. Multicolored autumn. It was her favorite season.

Sheba was waiting by the front door, whining. "What's the matter, old girl? George didn't come by to feed you?" George was the neighborhood handyman.

Her cat nuzzled up to her. It wasn't food she wanted, it was affection. Tired though she was, Emily knelt down on the top step of the porch and pulled her ancient friend close to her.

As she scratched behind Sheba's ear her eye automatically went to the big house up on the hill. There was not a light on in the whole house. Oh, Lord, Em thought. He's already moved away! What an idiot I am to let him escape! And then she grinned at herself. As if I could have kept him when he didn't want to be kept, she thought. The grin turned to a grimace as she stood up and stretched.

"Come on, girl," she called as she made for the front door. Sheba was instantly in front of her, as if barricading the door. "What's the trouble?"

The cat tried an acrobatic trick. She sat down in front of Em and wagged her tail at the same time. Em's fear quotient overflowed. She put one hand on the cat's ornate little collar. "Something's wrong?" Her cat hissed and showed claws.

Emily Sturtevant was no dunce. She knew the drill. If you think a stranger is in your home, waiting, don't go in. Call the police instead. Unfortunately the nearest telephone was inside her house, and she would not for all the tea in China go up the hill to use Brad's telephone. Not one chance!

"But we do have something in our favor," she whispered to Sheba. "The telephone is on the table just inside the front door. If we rush in I could dial the fuzz in a minute—only Taunton does not yet have the nine-one-one emergency number, and trying to dial eight-two-three five thousand in the dark might be pretty risky if there really is someone inside. Maybe you could fight him off while I dial?'' Her cat lay down on the porch floor and tried to hide her head under her paws. ''So much for bravery,'' Em muttered as she opened the door.

Two steps into the room, she knew for sure that something was wrong. There was a feeling of... fullness to the old living room, as if it were crowded with—ghosts? Sheba slipped by her, backed against her leg, and mewed. It was a sort of apologetic sound, as if the cat were saying, ''I know you're in here, and if you don't go away I shall raise hell again. Perhaps.''

''Brave animal,'' Em muttered. Sheba didn't notice the sarcasm. She offered another hiss.

''All right, I know you're in here,'' Emily announced. ''You'd better give yourself up. My cat is a famous attack cat.'' There was a deep male chuckle from the depths of the far dark corner. ''And I've got a gun,'' she continued. Another chuckle. ''Rob?'' Her voice shook just the slightest bit. ''Rob, are you trying to scare me?''

''And succeeded, haven't I?'' the voice said. It was muffled, hollow, and not at all like Rob.

''Never say that,'' Emily snapped. ''Come out into the light. I have the telephone in my hand and I'm about to dial the police. No more fooling!''

Emily was slowly backing toward the door. She had told nothing but lies so far. She had no gun, Sheba was not an attack cat, and Em was fumbling with both hands, and had not yet found the telephone.

Three things happened simultaneously. Em found the telephone but there was another warm hand before her; somebody snapped on the light switch; and Brad Colson, resting on his crutches, put one arm around her.

''Why, you—— Brad?''

''Why, me—Brad. What's the problem, Nurse Sturtevant? Surely a woman of your practical experience couldn't be—— No, now...just a minute, here. No hitting a patient."

"You're not *my* patient," she grumbled as she found herself being towed, one-handed, over against his steel chest. He has only one hand to use, she told herself hysterically. God knows what he'd do with two! Brad Colson stroked her hair, dug out the pins of her chignon, and let the whole mass fall to her waist.

"How's that?" he murmured.

Emily's fear had fled, and now her anger dissipated. It was such a warm comfortable place to be. "That's— fine," she said. "Fine!" She offered a weak laugh. "Would you believe, I thought it might be Rob, and he was angry with me? Stupid, huh?"

"If you believe in ghosts it probably wasn't stupid at all, love. Do you?"

"I—damn! I just don't know. How could you believe in haunts? And yet, yes, I've seen one, as plain as your nose. Maybe it's my imagination working overtime. Maybe—I just don't know. Yes, I believe in ghosts. There, I said it. Does that make you happy? What are you doing in my house?"

"One question at a time. Are you afraid of ghosts?"

"I—never thought about it that way," Em replied. "I suppose—I am."

"Admitting it is half the way to curing the fear," he pronounced. "Now where in the world is there a couch?"

"There's a love seat over in the corner," she said, and he could read the question in her sparkling eyes. "Why do you need one?"

"To make love on," he answered. "I can't seem to do a darn thing on these crutches."

I'm not going to fall for that old line, Em told herself. But I can't leave a patient standing there, I just have to help him over to the...and before she could think another thought they were at the love seat. He tucked her into it gently. Who's the nurse and who's the patient? Em asked herself as she sank into the soft cushions and gave a sigh of contentment.

"That's what I like," he said as he managed to squeeze in beside her.

Me too, Em thought. Look at us, packed in this seat like two sardines. It's big enough to hold two people comfortably. But not when one of them is Brad Colson. "I've been gone for a week," she murmured as she snuggled down on his shoulder.

"I know. I've been watching every day. Sheba wouldn't tell me a thing. Seems like six months, love."

Her words strangled her. So he *had* kept track, difficult though it was to believe. So why hadn't he done something about it? Love? What a lovely thought. He was about to move his arm around her shoulders, but she grabbed at the arm with both hands and held on for dear life. Not that she wouldn't mind having his arm around her, but, for the moment, all she wanted to do was hug him. Crazy thought, she told herself. I never ever felt that way about Rob, although I loved him with all my heart. Deep inside her a questioning voice said, Really?

"Oh, God," she muttered, and tried to hide her face against his chest. What am I saying? Rob has been my rock for years, even after he died. My true knight. I can't be thinking things against him. That's almost like high treason! She squeezed Brad with all her strength, and then broke away.

"So what are you doing in my house?" she challenged.

"Hiding out, lady. What's the matter?"

"I don't know what you mean. Nothing's the matter."

"Come off it," he teased. "I know very well what it means when I've got a bird halfway down out of the tree, and then all of a sudden she turns cold and flies away. What's the trouble?"

"Such experience," she muttered, and managed to squeeze another half inch away from him. "Now answer my question. Listen carefully. Why are you hiding in my house?"

"I've been here several days, love. Some person or persons unknown have bugged my work space. So I've been working here. Some little lovable person is trying to overhear everything I say, except when I'm in the bathroom. You wouldn't know anything about that, would you?"

"I——" Her guilty conscience began to nag at her. Her cheeks turned red. "I—perhaps I know something about it."

"Ah," he said, which was not the most helpful of comments.

"Ah?" she asked indignantly. "Is that all you've got to say?"

"No, not at all." Brad managed to get his arm around her and pulled her back toward him. Poor little bird, he told himself. She's so wound up inside with this ghost business that she's not able to think. Maybe I can help her.

Emily thought to fight, but then relaxed. It was enjoyable, being hugged by this massive man. But he's so wound up in his company problems that he hasn't had time to think, she thought. Maybe I can help him.

"It's that gift I brought you from your mother," she said. "The crystal pen set. It radiates. I put it down next to my nurse's pager, and it interfered with the system."

"Well, what do you know. My mother, huh? And how come you didn't tell me sooner?"

"At the time," Em said firmly, "I was angry with you. Now I'm not." He squeezed forward in the love seat and started to get up. "Where are you going now?"

"I'm going back to my house to smash a pen or two," he said. Her hand twitched at his sleeve, pulling him back. He landed with a thump, and the old cedar love seat complained.

"It seems to me," she drawled, "that you're a man of direct action rather than subtlety."

"Does it really seem so?"

"On the other hand, my father, who was a police captain in this town, always claimed that I was as subtle as they come."

He grinned down at her, and tapped her little nose with a big finger. "You're trying to tell me something," he said. "Don't sugarcoat it. I'm not the brightest man you ever met. I got where I am by hard work, not by intellect."

"Okay, then—you have to ask yourself why these people would want to bug your house. What use can this intelligence be?"

"Now that I can answer." He settled back again. "Colson Enterprises controls a great deal of property. I'm trying quietly to sell off some of the odd lines, and buy more heavily into organizations that could be integrated with present units. People would love to know beforehand just what I'm buying and what I'm selling. In fact, for a few days last week when they *did* know, prices on the stockmarket were running wild."

"And so you want to bust up the system?"

"Not grammatically correct," he chuckled, "but yeah."

"Silly. Here you've got a pipeline right into the enemy headquarters and you want to bust it up. Now if I were you——" She stopped and nibbled at her lower lip.

"Yes, if you were me?"

"If I were you," she said softly, "I'd keep this line working hard, feeding a few unimportant titbits down to your listeners until they think they've got everything secure, and then you feed them the biggest dose of false information that you can dream of."

"Lord," he sighed, "you are a conniver. What have I gotten into?"

"A cop's family," she assured him. "How'd you like to find out something else?"

"You love me?"

"Pipe dream," she told him, and moved as far away as she could get. Well, she told herself, there's no use giving the show away too soon. No, I don't love him— but maybe I'm getting close to the time when I might *consider* loving him. After all, he's nothing like Rob— nothing. And Rob is my guideline! "Come on," she added, "let's get a little action going."

"Right here is fine," he teased.

"Up," she snapped. "I don't do Friday-night games on the love seat. Out to my car."

"Now I don't know about that," he murmured in her ear. "I'm not too swell with car seats, either. Why don't we just amble upstairs and try a bed? I'm great in bedrooms."

"I'll bet you are." She had managed to squirm away from him. "But surely not with a broken leg?" Now she took a couple of steps away and began to tug her disordered blouse back in place. "Besides, that's not what I had in mind."

"I was afraid of that," he mourned. He gave her a questioning look.

"No," she stated. "I'm not going to get that close to you. Get yourself up by yourself."

"Nurses," he groaned. "Are they all born with icicles for hearts, or is that something they learn in the school, like a heart transplant?"

She turned around at the door and glared at him. He was swinging along across the rug as if crutching it were the natural thing to do. "That's all you think about," she muttered as she turned the knob. "Are all men like you? I'm something besides a body, you know."

"*Nice* body," he commented as he came up to her. She backed out of the door on to the veranda. "Surely Rob felt the same way?"

Her hand half rose in his direction. "You're not the man Rob was," she snarled. "He'd make three of you, Brad Colson. And he loved me for *who* I am, not *what* I am."

The little grin that seemed firmly fixed to his lips faded. "The *parfait* knight? Neither fault nor failure?"

"Of course." She stomped down the stairs. The wind caught in her loose hair and spread it all around her head. Brad stopped on the bottom step for a moment as she moved toward the car.

"That makes him almost impossible to compete with," he murmured. "Anyone with common sense would throw in his hand." Em heard. And was suddenly struck with a pang of regret.

Why did I say that? she pondered as she struggled with the car lock. Of course Rob wasn't perfect. Almost, but not perfect. And I . . . really want to—to what? To know Brad better? Well, that's a loose way of saying it, isn't it, dummy? Get in the car!

She slid behind the wheel and fumed at herself until Brad maneuvered himself around the car and climbed in the passenger seat.

"You do well with the crutches," she offered as a tentative apology.

"Ha! Crutches!" He added three or four words Em could not identify as he carefully maneuvered his damaged foot into the car. "Where are we going?"

"I learned something else about bugs," she said as she started the engine. "For every transmitter there must be a receiver. And this——"

"Hey, even I know that," he interrupted. "I'm not exactly stupid—just slow."

"I'm sorry." She looked over at him, her big green eyes sparkling with a speck of water in them. "I didn't mean to imply—I know you're not——"

"So go on with the story."

Em took a deep breath and drove the old car out into the road at a very slow pace. "What I meant to say is that, since the transmitter is very small, it can't be very powerful, and so the receiver has to be very close." She offered the information quickly and then clamped her lips closed before he could interrupt again.

"Now that I *didn't* know."

Emily stared at him in astonishment. Every boy in America knew things like that, but not Bradley? He must have read her mind, felt her doubts.

"What do you know about Colsons?"

"I—well—it's a big holding company. It has stores and factories. They sell things."

"Brilliant."

"I know it must be hard for you to believe," she said coldly, "but I grew up with a policeman, and studied nursing. It didn't give me a lot of time to go poking my nose into Colson stores. All I know for sure is that if anything comes from Colsons it's expensive. My mother told me that!"

"And now I owe *you* an apology." His voice had dropped a half octave, had become soft and deep and caressing. *Caressing?* Em shuddered. So I believe in ghosts and he has a caressing voice. I can't help but think that I'm losing all my marbles!

"Do you know why I like you, Emily Sturtevant?"

"No. I can't even imagine. My hair's a mess, I have freckles, and I'm not...well-constructed at all." And now tell me it's not true, she shouted at herself. Tell me!

"Men aren't always mad about hair and—er—construction, not as individual items," he said in a very conversational voice. As if none of that matters, she raged to herself. Ha! "And I do like freckles," he concluded. Em let her breath out in a massive sigh.

"What I like about you," he mused, "is that you're honest and sincere and hardworking..."

So was my grandmother, Em told herself. What kind of a compliment is that? She was so busy with her own commentary that she missed his last statement, and it sounded curiously like——

"What did you say? That last part?" She put her foot hard down on the brakes. The tires squealed them to a stop in the middle of the road as she turned to stare at him. "What did you say?"

He grinned at her, until his rugged face was all smile, with no room for anything else. "And you're sexy as hell," he repeated.

She sat quietly for a moment, both hands on the steering wheel, as she stared forward through the windshield. And then, "You must be out of your ever-loving mind."

"Possibly," he agreed. "You know the old saying? There's no accounting for taste?"

Emily gulped a time or two. She was having trouble with her breathing. "I think we'd better drive along," she told him, watching out of the corner of her eye.

He shrugged his shoulders. "With these cars that have the shift console between the two front seats there's not a hell of a lot else we could do."

"I wish you wouldn't swear so," she muttered, and shifted into gear. The car answered with a purr. Just ahead was a curve. She slowed to twenty miles an hour and they practically crept around the curve, which was something to be thankful for. Em always drove in the inside lane, as close to the edge of the road as was possible. And there was a blue panel truck, its roof festooned with antennae, pulled off to the side and projecting slightly out into the traffic lane.

Em froze for a fraction of a second. "Watch it," Brad roared at her. Her foot came down hard on the brake. The tires squealed and slipped on a patch of wet leaves, and the car skidded forward until its bumper just made contact with the parked truck. Not a tremendous bump, but enough to rock the panel truck forward an inch or two. Em could feel the perspiration drip down off her nose. She wanted badly to hit something—or somebody—to liberate her anger.

"That's the idea," she snapped at him. "Yell at me! You're one of those men who can't stand being in a car with a woman driver!"

"Not true." She looked across at him. He was breathing fast, and perspiration was dripping off his cheek as well. "You damn near creamed that truck," he said mildly. "And I'm not against women drivers. I'm against being in a car when anybody else but me is driving!"

"Chauvinist," she muttered. See Emily Sturtevant, she ordered herself bitterly. A nurse with years of experience. A woman of the world, accustomed to the ways of life and living, and scared half to death—either of what this man might say about her driving or of the near accident itself. I want to cry. And so she did.

It was probably the best thing she could have done. Up ahead of her the side door of the panel truck slammed back on its stops and an irate driver jumped down and strode towards Em's car, looking as if he were one of the avenging angels. He stuck his head in Em's open window and took a deep breath. But what did an irate male do about a female driver whose tears were running fast enough to raise the Taunton River by at least an inch?

"Hey, what the hell——?" he started out, and then paused. "Look, lady, there's no damn reason for you to run into me like that. You could have caused a lot of damage." She continued crying. He reached in the window with one ham hand, seized her wrist and shook it. Em was so startled that she shut off the tears.

"Hey, that hurts," she complained.

"It oughta," he grunted, and added another free twist. "Nothin' I hate worse than dumb women drivers."

Brad, who had slid down part way in his seat to avoid being recognized, stretched to his full size. "Say," he said mildly, "why don't you come over here and tell *me* about it?"

"No," Em interjected excitedly. "He can't walk. He has a broken foot!"

"Broken foot? Wait'll I get around there, buster, and you'll have a broken nose to go with it!" He was a big man. Em had failed to notice earlier, but now, as she watched him through the windshield, she could see the size of him, and the bulging muscles.

"Brad," she cautioned, but was too late. The man was around the car trying the locked door. Slowly, almost teasingly, Brad wound down his window.

"Now, wise guy," the other man said as he leaned in. He bulked up in the dark. His head seemed to fill the window, and his broad shoulders were just too wide to go through the open space. At least it seemed that way.

"The dame is a lousy driver. You oughta see she don't drive on the highways, Mac. Now it's going to——"

The conversation was cut off. Brad moved casually, one-handed. With a handful of shirt and sweater and neck all wrapped up in his closing fist he pulled the man inexorably into the car, whether his shoulders would fit or no. The man was gargling for breath when Brad began the lecture.

"You made a couple of mistakes," Colson said in that mildly deceptive tone. "You probably should never have gotten out of bed. And secondly, you should never have put a hand on my girl."

One more little additional twist of his hand, and the big man began to whimper.

"*My* girl," Brad repeated, and now his voice was harsh and cold. "Nobody talks tough to *my girl*. Not even me. You got that?" The big head, almost in his lap, managed an affirmative nod. "And you actually made her cry! By damn, I ought to take your head off and see what's inside."

"Please," Em pleaded as she tried to restrain Brad. "It wasn't all that bad. Really it wasn't."

"No? Then how come your wrist is all red? Hell, it's worse than I thought. I'm gonna beat up on this loser." With that Brad pushed against the strangled man, who bounced back out of the window, tumbled a time or two, and rolled down into the drainage ditch. A moment later he was up and running—away from Brad's side of the car.

"Now look what you've done," Brad complained sadly. "I can't possibly catch him now."

"But I . . . you shouldn't——"

"Of course I should," he growled. "Nobody puts the arm on *my* girl!"

Em sagged back into the driver's seat and cried some more. Tears because she was tired; tears because he had called her sexy; tears because the night was closing in and she wished she were at least fifty miles away. Tears because, although he had made many a remark earlier, this time he was so obviously angry—and telling the absolute and basic truth. *His girl!* Nothing flamboyant, just a straightforward statement. "Nobody puts the arm on *my* girl!" And she cried a little harder, because it had just struck her that she wasn't his girl at all, and she really *wanted* to be!

"Now, darling," Brad said. "Don't cry. The man is sorry he parked right where you wanted to drive. And don't curse. What would the children think?"

With that Emily's sorrowful tears turned to tears of anger, and flowed all the faster for that. All the children! That was going just two steps too far! What would the children——? Not just one. Some. What sort of a man would——? All the children. She thumped on the steering wheel with all her might. Brad slid over in his seat, as far away as he could get.

At the same time the blue van seemed to have reacquired its full crew. The motor roared in the silence of the night and the panel truck moved off down the road, its multiple antennae dancing a macabre waltz with themselves.

"You can turn off the waterworks now." Brad inched toward her and offered a massive handkerchief to dry her eyes.

"Not before I give you a good knock," she stuttered. "I've not been so angry in years. Darn chauvinists! If

God were not too busy right now I'd pray that She give you a case of shingles!''

''All right, if it will make you feel better, go ahead and hit me.''

''Darned if I will.'' She restarted the car's engine and wheeled around in an illegal U-turn. ''Why should I do something just to make *you* feel better?''

''Yes, there's that.'' In the darkness she could not quite see him clearly, but it sounded as if he were laughing at her. Laughing as he hung on to the door handle for dear life as she kicked her old car around the bends of Briggs Street with all the panache of a Le Mans driver.

She stopped in front of *his* house and blew the horn. A light came on in the front window, and after a moment Alfred appeared, pushing the wheelchair in front of him.

''And do you know what really aggravates me?'' Brad mused. With the car at a stop Em turned and looked at him. ''They're actually using my own trucks and equipment to bug me!''

Emily chuckled as she drove sedately down to her own house. He was some kind of guy, there was no doubt about that. What kind? The kind Emily Sturtevant liked, that was what. And with that she parked the car next to the house, hugged herself gleefully, and struggled to get out.

Sheba was waiting, not with her usual disdain, but excitedly, her tail wagging at ten to the second as she jumped up at Em, crying. ''Look, cat, if you don't stop that jumping I'll never get out of this car.'' Her cat gave her about twenty seconds of consideration and then started jumping again. But by that time Em had managed to get both feet on the ground, and she was home free.

She shook down her dress, brushed a careless hand though her hair, and headed for the porch. It was only then that she noticed the dark shadow on the veranda.

"Hello there, Miss—Sturtevant." The mass dissolved itself and became Mrs. Colson, mopping the top of her forehead with a handkerchief despite the cool autumn winds. "Hot, isn't it?"

"Not really. In fact there's a nip of fall in the air." Em climbed the stairs slowly. There's no reason to hurry, just to meet the chief villain—villainess?—of the piece, she thought. "What brings you here, Mrs. Colson? Surely not a social call?"

"Not really, but it could be. What makes you think it isn't?" the old lady probed.

"Because you haven't paid me, Mrs. Colson. I suppose your little 'gift' is working well?"

"What little——? Oh, that. Working? I don't know quite——"

"Come on," she said, chuckling. "You know darn well I don't mean that the pen writes well. So you had me plant a bug on Mr. Colson. How's it working?"

"Well, now, little lady, I hadn't expected you to——"

"My father was a police officer. I've seen bugs before. Now, about my money?"

"That's not what I came to see you about, Miss Sturtevant."

"Mrs. Sturtevant. And until I see the color of your money, Mrs. Colson, you have nothing else to see me about. Good night."

Colson's mother cleared her throat in the darkness, and then surrendered. "Money," she sighed. "The root of all evil. Could we possibly go inside? I feel—somewhat uncomfortable standing out here." It was almost pitch dark, but Mrs. Colson glanced around nervously, and pulled her short coat up closer around her neck.

"You've got that quote a little offside," Emily said. "The good book says that 'the love of money is the root of all evil.' Come in." She led the older woman up the stairs and into the house.

"No lights, please," Mrs. Colson cautioned. Em ignored the command and flipped the switch on one of the floor lamps.

"You can't have it both ways, ma'am." Mrs. Colson winced. "You don't want to stand outside in the dark, but you *do* want to stand inside in the dark. That doesn't make a lot of sense, and, since it's my house, we'll have a light."

Mrs. Colson's lips tightened as she looked for a chair the furthest distance from the windows that looked up the hill. Just to tease her Emily pulled the curtains back. "Ah," she commented, "our neighbor, Mr. Colson, is back. Now, about the money?"

"Yes, the money. Twenty, I believe we agreed." Her hand dived into her bag and came out with a checkbook and pen.

"For a successful businesswoman you have a lousy memory," Em said. "I, on the other hand, have a very good memory. Fifty, wasn't it?"

Mrs. Colson looked up at her in astonishment. "Never," she snapped. "Not ever. Twenty-five was the agreement." The matriarch's face was turning red as she flipped open her checkbook and started to write.

"Oh, no, none of that," Em said. "I wasn't born yesterday. This is strictly a cash and carry business. You know what your trouble is, Mrs. Colson? You don't seem to be willing to invest money to make money. That skinflint idea of business operations is for the birds. Maybe you'd like me to give you a course in how to *spend* money?"

Mrs. Colson choked, as if the idea stuck in her craw. There was a noise from upstairs that shook her out of it. "Someone's upstairs?" she asked as she returned her checkbook to an inside pocket and pulled out a roll of bills that would choke a horse.

"Nobody you need to pay any attention to," Em said. "That's my family ghost. I don't really think he cares about you or your son or anyone else, for that matter."

"Ghosts? Nobody believes in ghosts." Mrs. Colson peeled off a very small number of bills from the pile and handed them to her. Em, who had grown up in a family where every dollar was counted and recounted, returned an extra ten dollar bill to her.

"I know our agreement should have been for more than this." Em checked the bills again, and, having nowhere else at hand, tucked them down into the front of her bra. "But I'll let you get away with it this time." There was another noise from overhead. Mrs. Colson looked apprehensively at the stairs.

"You don't believe in ghosts?" Em used one hand to smother her giggle. "Even if he comes downstairs?"

"Not a chance," Mrs. Colson said firmly. "Now, Mrs. Sturtevant, that we've got the money situation out of the way, I wonder if you would be interested in another small favor——"

"At the same wage scale?" she interrupted.

"I—er. Perhaps we could discuss that later?"

"Perhaps we could, sir. What's the problem?"

"Well, as you've undoubtedly guessed, we're not getting as much information as we would like to have. On the other hand, we've noticed that all the help in Mr. Colson's house leave on the weekend. Now tomorrow is Saturday. Do you suppose you could prevail on my son to take you out to dinner tomorrow night?"

"Ah, a little more hanky-panky," Em said, grinning at her. "A little breaking and entering?"

"For his own good," Mrs. Colson insisted. "For his own good. As his mother, I approve of the whole affair."

"You do? What a strange woman you must be."

For the first time Mrs. Colson's face showed some reaction. "I love my son," she said bitterly. "I have a deep and abiding love for him. But I also have some large debts which must be paid off."

"An expensive hobby?"

"You—could say that, yes. I have made some... unfortunate investments—as has Brad himself. Mine is the mission to preserve the Colson enterprises, and to provide for me—for both of us in our older days."

Listen to that, Emily told herself, she's finally worked things around to where she's the good guy! Hurrah for motherly love! Brad's hobby is obviously buying sports cars for women like Evelyn. I just wonder what his mother's little hobby might be?

"You do interest me, Mrs. Colson." Emily walked over to the love seat and dropped down into it. The instant her back made contact with the seat she had a sudden flashback. Sitting on that love seat, squeezed in against the warm strength of Brad Colson! Her eyes went dreamy and for a moment his mother was miles away—until the old lady cleared her throat. Em jumped up. One could hardly connive, she told herself, while sitting in that *particular* chair.

"I think we perhaps might be able to deal," she said, "but I'm not sure about Saturday night. I need a little leeway. So let's say, if I can do it for Saturday night, you'll owe..." Em's mind raced like crazy. Dinner for two at the finest restaurant in town? Wine? A large tip? Music? "I couldn't possibly do it for less than a hundred dollars. If it has to wait until Sunday I'll give you a bargain. Ninety-five dollars. What do you say to that?"

"Piracy," Mrs. Colson muttered. "Pure piracy."

"Ah, but I've got the only game in town," Em chuckled.

"All right, all right," the old lady grumbled as she stood up. "Try to make it Saturday. I need all the time I can get."

"I'm sure you do." Em dimpled. "And now you have to rush off?"

"Not exactly," she said. "I don't hurry at other people's commands, young lady. It's the other way around with me."

"How satisfactory that must be," Em sighed. And at just that moment there was another thump from upstairs, and something heavy seemed to be rolling down the stairs.

"But I can't see anybody," Mrs. Colson whispered hoarsely.

"Of course not," Em said. "Luckily, you don't believe in ghosts, you said."

The old lady turned white, and moved more quickly than a woman of her weight could possibly go. The front door slammed behind her. Emily walked slowly over to the foot of the stairs and caught the heavy rubber exercise ball that had been pushed down the stairs. "Sheba, Mrs. Colson said good night," she called. "What the devil are you playing at now?"

Her cat sauntered down the stairs to the bottom step, sat down, and began to polish the fur between her claws. And when she was finished she came up to four feet, arched her back, and gave Emily a look which said, Well, you're only a girl—you can't be expected to know everything!

Emily, frustrated, watched her go, swaying like her namesake. At which the widow Sturtevant yelled after her cat, "I could have gotten a gerbil for a pet, you know!"

CHAPTER SIX

ALFRED met Em at the door almost as soon as her finger touched the bell. He was wearing a size-six frown. "It's Saturday," he said as he lifted his wristwatch up to where they both could read the dial. "Eight o'clock Saturday morning."

"There's something wrong with Saturday?" Emily had been up half the night constructing plots to fit, and finally struck on one that might do. Not perhaps the best answer, but an answer nonetheless. "That's a nice watch. Very accurate, I suppose," she said. The little man's right eye was twitching. Em scanned his face. At the beginning of their acquaintance Alfred had been a friendly sort of fellow, but now...?

"*We* don't arise at such an hour on Saturday," he said. Any more starch in his words and his backbone might have cracked. "I thought——" He broke off with an artificial cough.

"It's a lovely fall day," Em said innocently. "And Saturday morning is the best part of it. What was it that you thought?"

"To be honest with you, I thought Mr. Colson had given you your—*congé*, so to speak. Why don't you go away and come back next week? Thursday would be a good day. We plan to be in Plymouth on Thursday."

"Alfred, are you guarding the door, trying to give me the brush-off?"

The little man gave her a doleful look. "Trouble," he said. "I knew you'd be trouble. That long hair; those green eyes. The master and I have enjoyed a pleasant relationship for some time, Mrs. Sturtevant. I would not have our confidences broken by some . . . interfering—er—nurse. Surely there are a dozen men in this area who would want to—er—would want to? Why pick on Mr. Colson?''

Emily gave him a sunny smile and moved closer. She took his arm and coaxed him into sitting beside her on the stairs. "I don't think you understand, Alfred. I have no intention of—breaking up your wonderful friendship. My relationship with Mr. Colson is purely platonic."

"Yes, and I've heard that pigs in Taunton fly," he muttered. "The poor man has come unglued, miss. He sits and stares off into space and talks to himself. I don't know what to make of it, because whenever he tells you something you answer him back. And you're not there!"

"Now, now," she teased. "And I'm not there? How could that be?"

"There are some as say your house is haunted," the little man said solemnly. "Or is it because you're a witch?"

"No," she sighed, thinking that indeed *someone* was coming unglued. "No, I'm a registered nurse. It's not *quite* the same thing as being a witch. But I don't see why you are so concerned. Why, he told me himself that he was just an average man who didn't believe in ghosts and witches."

"Average?" Alfred snorted. "He's about as average as a hungry barracuda. A woman like you—a fine upstanding woman of means—you ought to be careful about what you say or do around Mr. Colson!"

"Careful?" She looked down at his anxious face and grinned. "You've never known a woman as careful as I am when around your Mr. Colson. But still—I think I'll hang around for a time."

Alfred glared up at her. "Is it money? Mr. Colson and I have a very satisfactory arrangement. The hours are short, the work is light, and the pay is—more than satisfactory. The one thing *we* do not need is a female interloper. I'd be willing to pay you a thousand dollars, Mrs. Sturtevant. From my own savings, mind you."

"For which grand amount I'll be required to do what?"

"Go away," he muttered. "Just go away."

"Strange," she said, laughing. "I've been broke for years. Now, within the space of a week, all kinds of people seem to want to give me money! I'll consider your offer, Alfred." She rose gracefully and tried to slip by him. He put a pleading hand on her wrist.

"Please?"

"Believe me, Alfred," she said, looking compassionately down at the hand that trembled on her wrist. "I've a couple of things to say to Brad. Nothing more. I will be doing him some good. You'd like that, wouldn't you? I would be helping him to regain control of his corporation. Surely nothing could be nicer than that?"

"Of course," he agreed, but the doleful look on his face indicated otherwise. "He's in the kitchen, Miss Emily."

"Mrs.," she reminded him, and walked by into the house. Her heels tapped on the polished hardwood floor, but nothing else seemed to be stirring. She paused to investigate each door as she passed down the hall.

"Brad? Bradley?"

She found him, in the living room cum study, both elbows on the table, his chin cupped in the palms of his hands, surrounded by computers—staring out of the window that overlooked her own house. "Brad?"

"I told you I didn't want any," he mumbled. "Go away."

"That seems to be the order of the day around here," she answered. "But I'm not going." Em looked around. The brandy bottle was on the table. A fresh bottle, still sealed. Next to it was his bottle of painkillers. "Brad?" She rattled his shoulder and broke the trance.

"What the hell are——? Emily!"

"Right the first time," she answered. "What's going on? Booze and pills at the same time?" Her professional fingers glided down to his wrist and took his pulse. "That combination will send you galley-west, Bradley."

"Galley-west?"

"Yes. Over the hill."

He shrugged his shoulders as if trying to shake himself back to reality. "For your information, Em Sturtevant," he said, "I haven't had a drop of liquor in the past seventy-two hours. You told me about the pills. I'm not so stupid as to neglect professional advice."

"Well! I am surprised."

"So am I," he said glumly. "Your pills leave a lot to be desired."

She gave him a teasing half grin. "Like what?"

"Like this, damn you," he snapped. And before she could catch her breath he had seized her by both wrists, swung her around, and pulled her down into his lap. "Like this," he muttered as his warm, moist lips moved in on hers and shut down all her awareness systems! Emily struggled for a second. Pro forma, of course. And then she relaxed against him.

His lips nibbled at hers, his tongue chased across and into her mouth. A burning sensation attacked her, centering, of all places, just below her navel, and then moving upward at lightning speed, creating havoc in her no longer disciplined mind. When he released her she lay there in his arms, exhausted. "Oh, my," she muttered.

"Yes, I could agree with that," he returned. She tried to get up. His arm pulled her back.

"Don't do that," she said, but lay back against his comforting shoulder. "I'm not one of your women." But I wish I were, she told herself. I really wish I were. Oh, not for a complete affair. Just for another minute or two.

"It wouldn't take long for you to join my harem," he said. This time she was stung with indignation, and managed to sit up.

"Don't you just wish it," she snapped.

"More than anything else I can think of at the moment," he returned.

"At the moment? Because I'm the nearest woman in your world?"

"Because you're the only woman in my world," he returned. "Now stop fishing around for compliments. What brings you here? After last night I thought I had become *persona non grata.*"

See, she told herself, he really isn't perfect! I'm wearing my thoughts all the way across my face, and he can't read them! Thank God. Or maybe my freckles are covering everything else?

"I've never seen a sexier woman," he said. And then the sarcasm came back into his voice. "But of course you wouldn't think of that—not at this time of day— would you?"

"Got it in one," she mused. "No, I——"

"Well, when you're ready," he offered, "just call."

"What I came for," she told him angrily. "Would you mind getting your head out of the gutter and listen?" With a loud exclamation mark.

He threw up both hands in a defensive gesture. "I'm listening."

"Yes, and so are they," Em told him as she struggled to her feet and reached for the pen set. "Wait," she mouthed as she danced out of the room and set the bug up carefully in the kitchen next to the waste-disposal unit, which was grinding away for dear life.

"Now then," she told him as she hurried back. "How'd you like to take me out to dinner tonight?"

His eyes lit up. "Dinner? You and I? And then afterward?"

"Whoa up," she snapped at him. "Just dinner. On me. I'm standing the treat."

"Now that's a fine offer," he told her. "I'm not broke, you know. We could go Dutch."

"You'll find this hard to believe," she said, "but I have suddenly come into some money. Not a terrible lot, but enough to stand a good meal."

"It's a date," he enthused. "You'll pick me up about eight?"

"Look, it's not a date," she insisted. "This is a...business arrangement." Brad's chin dropped a mile.

"A business dinner?" he grumbled. "That's like kissing my sister."

"You'll enjoy it," she assured him. Her wandering had brought her back to his side, and her fingers were unable to resist. She watched as they ran through the silky hair, toyed with his non-lobed ears. Kissing his sister? "You don't have a sister!"

He grinned up at her obvious indignation. "But it sounded good, didn't it? I've used that phrase with many a woman. They all liked it."

"Damn you!" She stamped her foot, took a deep breath, and proceeded to tell him all about her plot for the evening, all at flank speed—until she ran out of breath, stopped, glared at him again, and said, "So there!"

"Indeed. So there," he chuckled. "Okay, I'll set up the trap. And perhaps a camera or two, just to see what the response is."

"Don't overdo it," she cautioned. "This trap mustn't look like a trap. Now, I have to go over to the Plaza to do some food shopping, before Sheba goes on strike."

"You could kiss me one more time," he offered.

"A girl would be a fool to do something——"

She had no idea how it happened, but there she was, leaning over, her lips voluntarily touching his. And not until she got back home did she reason it all out. "I'm mad," she told Sheba. "Totally, unequivocally mad. He's just the sort of man I want no part of. It must be my late nights, huh?" Her cat offered a little meow and nudged her out to the car. Wise animals like Sheba learnt to keep track of shopping-for-food days. It was a survival technique animals learnt as soon as they discovered that their mistresses were a little flaky.

Dinner with Brad. Dinner with Brad. What in the world can I wear? Benjamins. Not necessarily an ultraclass restaurant, but almost the best that Taunton had to offer. And her closet was filled with rejects and darling little shifts that even secondhand stores would not accept. "God," she muttered. Sheba, just in from chasing squirrels, mewed and lay down at her feet. There was, of course, one dress, almost new. Hesitantly she pulled it off its hanger and took it over to the light. A crisp challis jumper in soft breezy rayon with a double-breasted vest top, in a delightful Paisley print, worn over a boat-neck long-sleeved white blouse. Not the most inspiring dress for cocktails and after—but then again, she told herself firmly, this is strictly a business meal and there isn't supposed to be any "and after"!

After the arguments with herself about dresses, a considerable debate about makeup, a hurried dash to the kitchen to feed Sheba, she barely made it to the Colson front door by eight o'clock. Brad was sitting on the porch. Somebody had resurrected an ancient canvas swing, and he was sitting there, propelling himself back and forth with his good leg.

"Coming?" Em leaned out of the car window and yelled again.

"My mother always told me that when someone took me out on a date she had to come to the door," he yelled back. With a groan Em climbed out of the car and bounded up the stairs.

"You can think of the darnedest things," she told him.

"Can't I? I can't get up."

"What in the world...?"

"This swing is great for sitting down in," he complained. "But every time I try to stand up it—it swings. Give us a hand up, there's a good girl."

"You've been associating with Alfred far too long," she told him, but bent in the gathering darkness and slipped an arm under his. "Now, altogether, buster, on the count of three. One...two—— Damn you, Brad Colson!"

On the count of two he had flexed his not inconsiderable muscles and pulled her down on top of him. The swing rattled and rolled, he swept her up into his lap, and kissed the tip of her nose. "Don't move like that," he complained. "A fellow can't hardly kiss a wiggly girl."

"A fellow had darn well better knock it off," she returned fiercely. "I'm wearing my very best go-to-dinner outfit. You picked a terrible time to play Tarzan. I'm not joking—Mr. Colson."

"Spoilsport," he muttered as he turned her loose. She shook herself as Sheba might, getting her dress to fall as it should, and before she could offer him assistance he was up, crutches and all.

"That didn't require much help," she observed. "Are we through playing games?"

"For the moment," he chuckled. "After you, princess."

The long drive through town and down to Bay Street went by without another word spoken between them, although she could see out of the corner of her eye that his hand was moving sneakily across the bench seat, aimed directly for her thigh. "Down, boy," she told him, slapping at the wandering hand. But there was no need for further words. He had been moving too slowly for the distance they had to drive. She pulled off the road into the parking lot on Bay Street, jammed on the brakes to shake him up a little bit, then set the emergency brake with a determined yank. "Benjamins," she announced.

"Looks like a house, not a restaurant," he commented as he worked his way out of the car and rested for a moment in his crutches.

"It is," she teased him. "Well, to be exact, it was several of them. They converted them." They went in through the front door to find themselves facing the *maître d's* desk. Behind it a colorful lounge and bar were half full, and the conversations of the crowd blended into a subtle roar. A massive stone fireplace spread light if not heat throughout. And behind the lounge was an almost empty patio.

"Upstairs they have private rooms," she told him.

"That's for me," he said, grinning.

"Wait just a minute," she announced. "They're not those little cubbyholes. You're not going to get me into one of those affairs. We came to eat, not to play games."

"I knew there was something rotten about your character," he announced as he followed her through the lounge and out into the glass-enclosed patio. Background music sounded from some concealed source. Chatter floated on the peaks of the music. Emily followed the *maître d'* to one of the corner tables in the rear. "Too cold for eating outside," she told him. "Now if it were summertime—— Watch out for your leg!"

"Don't tell me to watch out," he growled as he collapsed into the chair that the waiter held. "From here on in, *you* look out, lady."

Ignore that, she told herself. Make believe he never said it. "I'll have a daiquiri," she told the hovering wine waiter. "My—er—father can't drink alcohol. Perhaps you might bring him a Virgin Mary?"

"Why, you——" he sputtered as the wine waiter walked away. "Father? I'll father you, young lady. And don't you forget it."

"Don't threaten me," she said, but it was hard to suppress the giggles. "You are being done good to, Mr. Colson. Can't you realize that? Did you get the cameras set up?"

"Don't change the subject," he snapped. "Nurses! Bah! No wonder so many patients die."

"Drink your Virgin Mary," she said solicitously. "There's a good fellow!"

"A good fellow," he muttered. "If my aides in the corporation heard that they'd die laughing. A good fellow, indeed!"

"But your business aides are just not around," she retorted. "Now you can relax and be your normal self."

"I am my normal self," he growled. "What you see is what you get!"

"Not me." She imitated a shudder. "I wouldn't have you baked on a bed of seaweed and sprinkled with paprika." A pause while she debated with herself. "I don't understand how you can be so overcrowded by women. Do you tell them all the same thing?''

"The very same." A slow grin was spreading across his face as he leaned closer. "They all go for it. It's that primitive-man thing that gets them all. And it helps not to have to remember all their names.''

"They do an especially good steak here,'' she announced primly as she tried to change the subject. Such a macho pain in the neck. Such a ... Why any woman would fall in love with him is hard to see, she told herself. Just an average Joe, according to himself; or a financial genius, according to Alfred. Whom could a woman believe these days? She handed him a copy of the menu. He was laughing at her now, over the top of the folder.

When their waiter came up he ordered, rapid fire, for both of them. Em started to protest, and then strangled the reflex. He might very well bite her head off if she objected. Except for one thing. "No. I want mine well done," she demanded. "I can't stand the sight of blood on my steak!"

"And you a nurse," he quipped. "Now, tell me about yourself, little Emily——"

"Sturtevant," she prompted.

"Nonsense. What was your maiden name?"

"Sullivan," she replied. "And you? What was your maiden name?"

"I——" he started to sputter, and then caught himself. "I see, Miss Sullivan. What's good for the goose, huh? Have you decided which yet?"

"Which what? All you're doing is confusing me."

"A short memory," he chuckled. "I offered marriage or a fancy affair. Made your choice yet?"

"Damn you!" Her capable little fist slammed down on the table. The couple next to them turned to stare.

"I take choice three," she muttered at him. "None of the above."

"Not quite ripe yet," he commented. "Well, we'll just take a little more time, shall we? How are things going along with your ghost?"

Caught short, Emily swallowed hard. There was a tear forming in her left eye. "I—haven't seen him lately," she reported. Her voice trembled just the tiniest bit. He reached across the narrow table and covered her shaking palm. "But how do I know whether it's a real ghost or a hallucination? It could very well be all in my imagination."

"I think it's real," he said. "When you describe it it sounds as if you think he's real. And, if that's so, who am I to be a doubter? He must have been quite a man."

"Yes, he was." Em took refuge in a tissue for just a moment. "The finest man I've ever known. I don't think I could find another like him."

"No, but then again you wouldn't want another *like* him, Em."

"I . . . suppose you're right. I'm not really looking for a man, but if I were—well, Robert was as fine a one as you'll ever see coming down the Pike."

"I'm sure he was," Brad said as he patted her hand. "But tell me something about yourself as well. Where did you meet this prodigal?"

"Right here in Taunton. I was born in the house two blocks from yours, grew up in the area, graduated from Coyle-Cassidy High School, and then went over to Morton Hospital for my training in nursing. I met Rob when we were in the second grade. He was a terrible tease in those days, but the day after I got my cap we were married."

"And your dad was a policeman?"

"He preferred to be called a cop. Yes. He never made high rank on the force, but he was a good cop, and people respected him. A heart attack killed him. That's one of the big problems of police work. It's heavily stressed. The older a man gets the more stress he faces. But no matter what his age he's expected to chase down young punks, to handle drunks, to face guns. More policemen die of heart diseases before they retire than get to settle down on their pensions. Which aren't all that much, by the way."

"So you've known two good men in your life?"

"Yes. My dad, and Rob—and then there's you. You're quite a man yourself, Brad Colson. And what do you think of that?"

"I'm totally whelmed," he chuckled. "Not over-whelmed, not underwhelmed, just plain whelmed."

"Now tell me about you," she demanded.

The waiter interrupted them by bringing dinner. It looked and smelled and tasted, "Just fine," he reported as he sliced the steak with his fork. "Just fine. Yours?"

"Maybe just a pinch undercooked, but edible," she reported. "But now how about you?"

"Me? Boring, average me," he said as he continued his attack on his steak. "Born in Wellesley, went off to Groton, and then to college. Kicked over a few wild oats in my time, and then, when my father died suddenly, I felt I had to move in on the corporation before my mother spent us into the poor farm."

"Yeah, boring, average man," she teased. "Alfred tells me differently. Alfred talks about barracudas in the financial seas. Schemers. Things like that. What college?"

"Who, me?"

"Come on, now."

"A small engineering college." He had managed to demolish his steak, and was about to destroy the baked potato when he peered at her and saw the look on her face. "So, all right, Massachusetts Institute of Technology."

"Just a small engineering college," she mocked. "Lord, are you ever loose with the truth!"

"Come on, now," he protested. "I may evade the truth now and again, but only for the good of the community! Go ahead, ask me a question. Any question. I'll guarantee you get the whole truth."

"I'll bet," she said. "The whole truth?" He nodded. "Why do you keep trying to sell me on that bluff man-about-town personality?"

"I'm shy?"

"Yeah. Of course. Did you order me any dessert?"

The waiter interrupted them again. "Mr. Colson? There's a telephone call for you. The caller says it's urgent. In the telephone booth across the room."

"Take it," Em encouraged him. "You might come up with a better answer by the time you get back."

"Women," he muttered as he turned his chair away and struggled up on his crutches. "Don't go away."

"I won't. This is more fun than emptying bedpans." He gave her an unbelieving look and then crutched his way around the perimeter of the room. And that, Em told herself, is one wonderful man. Conceited, underhanded, but wonderful. If only a woman knew exactly what's going on inside his brain. Marriage or an affair? How can I believe he means either one of them—or both?

"Young lady."

Em, who had been daydreaming while dawdling with her chocolate mousse, looked up in surprise. A portly gray-haired woman wearing more gold necklaces than the law ought to allow. Only the number of ruffles on her dress exceeded the number of chains. Mrs. Colson, dressèd to kill.

"I need to talk to you."

"I—I'm afraid this isn't the best time," Em responded. "Perhaps tomorrow? I could manage a free hour on Sunday, if you have some physical problem."

"I don't have a physical problem," the dowager told her. A waiter, responding to a snap of her fingers, came over to help with a chair. "You know me. Let's not have any running around the bush."

"But—we've already talked," Em wailed. "You're Bradley's mother, and you have an interest in his business, and I thought we had everything straightened out."

"Well, we didn't," the matriarch snapped. "When you were his nurse it did seem we had come to some agreement. But now I learn that you—for some strange reason—think he's going to marry you!"

"Perhaps you need to check your sources," Em retorted icily. "It takes two to tango. I have no more reason to want to marry your son than I would like to fly to the moon!"

"Then why do you find it necessary to ruin me?"

"Me?"

"Don't act innocent, young lady. You. Why are you doing your best to turn my son against me?"

"Why, I haven't—me?"

"It's no use dodging. My son told me that you are the reason why he can't give me any more money. How in the world do you think I can live on a pittance like that? Nine thousand dollars a month! I ask you, who could live on such a sum?"

"As you say, a pittance," Emily murmured. "But what does it have to do with me?"

"You—why, you—you know what it has to do with you. How can Bradley give me more allowance when he's spending all he has on a trollop like you? Look at that new convertible. And all those clothes. And your incessant demand for money! You think I don't know? You're even blackmailing Alfred. I know, believe me."

Do you really? Emily thought. My convertible? Good Lord, that car of mine is eleven years old. And all these lovely clothes? She could not help but smile as she fingered the smooth flare of her jumper. What was it—fifty-five dollars at Filenes? But blackmailing Alfred? How could that be?

"Alfred?"

"Alfred. You tried to blackmail him, and when he wouldn't pay up you struck him down in cold blood! Don't think I don't have my sources, young lady. And my son also. I have word that you were boasting about spending *his* money. All sorts of money just to entertain you. Well, you little fool, he's just leading you on. Just as soon as he gets you in his bed he'll close his wallet! Don't deny it!"

I can't deny it, Em told herself. In a way I'm also blackmailing you, Mrs. Colson. And you're going to pay the tab here tonight. But that's more than I want you to know at the moment. "I see you know even more than I do," she murmured. Mrs. Colson broke out a triumphant grin.

"Of course I know," the dowager said, preening herself. "Mothers always do."

Emily, who was as much for patriotism and motherhood as any other Taunton resident, smiled back. "Just what is it that you want me to do?" she asked.

Above the chatter, the occasional clash of a dish or two, the background music, Mrs. Colson provided an echo for an answer. "Go away," she said fiercely. "Go away."

"But I can't do that," Em protested. "I've lived in this town all my life. I can't just pick up and leave. I have a living to make."

"Yes, you can. I know it might be a problem for you, but if you had...money?" Em sat back in her chair. Look at that, she thought. People are just lining up, eager to give me money. Why didn't I discover this little trick five years ago? It certainly beats nursing hands down! And what do I say to the mean little old lady? She can't live on nine thousand a month? What a terrible strain that must be!

"How much money?"

The old lady blinked, then pulled up her massive bag from the floor. And that set Em's conclusion in place. The bag demonstrated that this was a Cadillac lady. In fact, the bag was big enough to *contain* a Cadillac.

"I could perhaps offer you——" a brief pause while Mrs. Colson fumbled through her purse "—five thousand dollars?"

"And all I have to do is go away?"

"That's all," the dowager agreed. "And stay away, of course. Well?"

"I'd have to think that over," Em said. "Perhaps you could call me tomorrow?" She looked into her own thin little bag and pulled out a business card. "There's my telephone number."

"Yes," the old lady decided. "I'll call you tomorrow." And with that she got up and scuttled off across the restaurant like a scorpion looking for someone else to sting. Mrs. Colson was hardly out of sight before her son came crutching it back to the table, a disgusted look on his face. Em, seriously considering recipes for boiling in oil, got up to help him with his chair.

"Something went wrong at the scene of the crime?"

"You wouldn't believe," he muttered. "I need a shot of the hard stuff."

"Not a chance," she told him.

"Say, who was that woman you were talking to?"

"Oh, you saw her, did you?"

"Just out of the corner of my eye. Some patient of yours?"

"Not quite," Emily said in as sweet a voice as she could manage. "She *said* she was your mother."

"Oh, God," Brad Colson muttered. "Waiter! A double Scotch please. My mother?"

"That's what she said, among other things."

"What other things?" Said tentatively, as if he really didn't want to ask, but didn't dare not to.

"Oh, you know, the usual stuff. About how you can't afford to give her any more money because of that new car you bought me. Oh, and all those clothes and things. You remember? She said you told her yourself. Did you have anything else you wanted to say?"

"Why the hell does that waiter take so much time? I only ordered a double Scotch, for cryin' out loud."

"Guilty, huh?"

"Em—there are two sides to every question, you know."

"As best I can figure out, three. Make a practice, do you, of spreading the truth around sparingly?"

His drink came at just the right time. Came and was thrown back down his throat as if he had just come out of the desert. He coughed, and his eyes watered.

"Em—it's a hard thing to do, to call your mother a liar. The truth is that I've never said a word about you to anyone in my family. I never had any desire to mix their sort of life with yours. So no, I never, ever said a thing to my mother, and especially I did not tell her that

I couldn't increase her allowance because of you." He leaned forward over the table and put the weight of both his mesmerizing eyes on her. "My mother has a problem. She's a compulsive gambler. She needs treatment, but she can't get it until she's willing to. You have to believe me, Em. I'm not the nicest man you ever met up with, but I'm not that low-down either."

So in the end, Emily told herself, it comes down to the same old problem. Whom do you trust? Brad or his mother? Is there any *other* evidence? Certainly you saw with your own eyes that Evelyn has the convertible. And she dresses like a daughter of the House of Windsor. Whom do you believe? Just one word, one refusal, and you lose Brad forever. Do you want that? A vision flashed through her mind. Herself, walking down a narrow dirt road that led to nowhere, with storm clouds in all directions, a terrible despondency beating on her mind, and a following of twisted ghosts to haunt her. Forever?

"No," she half whispered as she drew his hand across the table and pressed it against her cheek. "I believe you, Brad. But I could have made a fortune if I *didn't* believe."

His sigh was a gust capable of rattling windows. She could see the perspiration gathering on his forehead. And then he relaxed, leaning back in the chair.

"Our trap didn't work," he said, shaking his head dolefully. "He turned out to be the most inept burglar in the world. Alfred finally had to slip down and unlock the front door for him, and then—well, we'd better be on our way and see what can be rescued."

"Poor Alfred." But she was unable to suppress the giggle. She treasured his hand against her, unwilling to turn him loose. "So what happens next?"

"That's what we have to figure out. As far as I know, Alfred has the culprit locked up in the kitchen cupboard, waiting for further instructions."

"Poor Alfred."

"Poor Alfred hell. I mean—damn—I mean...oh, well, you know what I mean. How do you suppose my mother knew we'd be here tonight?"

"She followed us? Or a wire tap?" Em suggested. "I used my telephone to make the reservation."

"Is that legal? I mean the wire tap."

"No, but what else is new?"

"I don't know, do I?" he returned. "What do we do next?"

"You're asking me?"

"Who else do you think I could get to help out? I never knew what scheming really was until I met you, Emily Sturtevant. What do we do next?"

Em studied him in the dim light of the restaurant. A tall, virile, pleasurable man, looking at her with his head cocked to one side, waiting. "Well," she said, "why don't we...?" And her mind went back into high gear.

CHAPTER SEVEN

THEY went out into the rainy night. A dismal, thin sort of rain that blanketed all of New England. The streets were almost deserted. The few street lights gleamed intermittently, and traffic lights swayed in the gathering breeze. "Careful," Emily warned. "With the leaves and all it'll be slippery."

"Mother hen," Brad grumbled. When he came to a stop beside the car she wrapped her hands around his right arm and hugged him. "What was that for?"

"Does there have to be a reason?" she asked. "I just felt like it. C'mon, climb in." She held the car door open, and when he ducked his head she thought he meant to climb in. Instead he stopped long enough to kiss her. A warm—interesting—kiss, that left her flustered as he chuckled and slipped into the seat. As she walked around the car her mind boggled.

So when she was finally in the driver's seat she asked, a little breathless, "What was that about?"

"Not a thing," he answered. "I just felt like it. Does there have to be a reason?"

All of which left her with a sort of empty feeling in the pit of her stomach as she stared glumly out of the windshield.

"We're not going to sit here in the rain, I suppose," he supposed.

Emily muttered a word or two under her breath, started the engine, and wheeled down Bay Street as if the hounds of hell were after her. He only protested once—when she came up in front of his house with the brakes clamped on and skidded a good forty feet before they came to a stop.

"You should qualify for Monte Carlo," he said as he reached shakily for the door handle.

And the best she could think of for a response was, "Oh, shut up!" Which he did. He brushed off her offer of help, using his crutches with skill as he went up the path and onto the porch. Emily followed behind with as big a guilty conscience as one mind could encompass. Alfred waited for them with the door half open.

"Ah, Alfred. Where is the guilty culprit?"

"In the kitchen, sir. Locked in the closet."

"Not making any attempt to run off?"

"No. He seems to be a sensitive fellow. Somehow or another he has the impression that this house is haunted as well as Miss Emily's place."

"And he's bothered by that?"

"Shivering and shaking, sir. Do come and see." And then, as he stepped aside, a very shivery acknowledgment. "Mrs. Sturtevant." Alfred led the column down the hall; Emily stopped long enough to shut the front door and lock it. And then stopped again. From outside on the porch she could hear an extremely plaintive complaint. Sheba had finally decided to come up and join the crowd. Em opened the door just an inch or two, and the cat streaked by her and headed for the kitchen at full speed.

"Just whose pet *are* you?" she tossed after the cat, and got no response.

The men were waiting for her in the kitchen. Brad had sunk into one of the high-backed wooden chairs, and Sheba was already coiled up in his lap. Alfred stood at the back of Brad's chair, doing his best to keep out of range of the cat's claws.

Well, what a lovely family arrangement, Emily thought bitterly as she came into the room. Colson and his faithful man Alfred, and my cat! "Sheba," she called, "get down. Mr. Colson is allergic to cats!"

"Oh, I am?"

"You am," she snapped. Sheba paid her no attention at all. Instead the heavyweight cat shifted around to a more comfortable spot and began to purr. All of which did nothing to reduce Em's tension. "Where's the prisoner?"

Alfred gestured toward the cupboard door. Em strode over to it and turned the knob. "Why, you didn't even lock it," she said disgustedly.

"Well, I *thought* I did."

Em gave him a frosty look and took one step into the rather deep cupboard. Something rattled in front of her. She stopped in her tracks and moaned softly. Sheba rattled her claws on the linoleum as she scooted by her mistress and plunged into the darkness. A scream of terror floated up from near the floor. Em, trying valiantly to hang on to her nerves, backed out into the light. "Come out of there," she ordered. Chased out by the cat behind him, the man rolled over and over on the floor until he was out in the middle of the kitchen, where he came up to his knees.

Sheba, in her best attack-cat tradition, reared up on her hind legs and slashed the air with her claws. The man huddled down, covering his face with both hands.

"All right, all right," Brad said. "Both of you, knock it off!" His deep, vibrant voice stopped both cat and man in midstream. Sheba shrugged her shoulders, then leaped up into Brad's lap and began to preen. The poor little man on the floor hesitated, sat up, and then gradually removed his hands, as if he had been playing "peekaboo" with the gathering.

"And who, in the name of all that's holy, are you?"
Brad leaned forward to study the specimen. Alfred shook
his head. Sheba moved an inch forward, as if she were
about to pounce, but did nothing.

Emily said, "Hello, Ralph. Isn't it rather late for you
to be out?" Mrs. Colson's secretary gulped and looked
as if he wanted to throw up.

"You know this . . . person?" Brad looked over at her
in surprise.

"An old drinking friend," Em said as she offered the
man on the floor a big smile. "Ralph is a nephew of
your mother. And serves as her secretary, I believe? You
don't know the administrative staff?"

Ralph nodded. Or perhaps he didn't. His head moved
up and down, but that could easily have been the result
of the shivering over his entire body. Em decided not to
pursue the problem. "And Ralph is married to Mabel,
whoever she is," she added thoughtfully.

"How charming," Brad interjected. "A family affair."
He jerked a thumb in Alfred's direction, and nodded
toward the chair on the opposite side of the table. It
required a moment or two for the stricken man to get
settled. His face was as white as a sheet; his hands still
trembled.

"Brandy," Brad ordered. Em watched out of the
corner of her eyes as Alfred seemed to disappear, only
to reappear instantly with a brandy snifter in his hand.

"Drink that," Brad admonished. Before the words
were out of his mouth the glass was empty. Alfred disappeared again, and when he returned the glass had been
refilled. Ralph sipped a couple of times, then wrapped
both hands around the glass.

"Now then," Brad started off.

"The ghost? That cat?"

"That cat is nothing but a cat," Emily assured him. He looked up at her, disbelieving.

"And you're the witch," Ralph said. "I don't know which is worse, the witch or the ghost!"

"Pay them no mind," Brad interrupted. "Does Mabel know you're here?"

Ralph's teeth positively chattered. "I...no. And I hope she——"

"Not to worry," Brad said comfortingly. "Why don't you just tell us what you were doing here?"

Ralph leaned back against the chair and tried to relax. "I—he—I came up to the house and...came in, and——"

"And broke in," Emily said. "Breaking and entering in the night time, for the purpose of committing a felony. We're talking *beaucoup* years in the slammer, Ralph."

"Finish your brandy," Brad advised. "We're not all out to get you. It's bad enough that you're a family member. I just don't remember which side of the family——"

"My mother..." Ralph babbled. "Your mother's second cousin."

"Well, we shouldn't persecute you for that." Ralph's glass was refilled. He raised and tilted it and the liquid disappeared, only to be refilled instantly by the watchful Alfred. "So now, then, what were you looking for?"

"A buy list," Ralph almost whispered. "Mrs. Colson was certain you would have a buy list of all the stocks you wanted to purchase just as soon as you regained control of the company."

"Now why would she want to know that? Try a little more brandy, Ralph."

Ralph did. His cheeks were red, and he spoke with wine-induced bravado. "Because then we were going to buy up that stuff before you could, and then make you buy from us at an inflated price! We'd make a bundle!''

"Tch,'' Brad said. "Dishonesty too. What *would* Mabel say?''

"That's...that's not dishonesty,'' Ralph said. He was beginning to have trouble with his "h'' sounds. Dishonesty came out as "dish-onesty.'' "That's jus' good business. Do unto others before they do unto you! You know that. M'brother, he said he learned it all from you!''

"Ah, he works for the company too? In that case he probably did,'' Brad replied. "Well, that puts a different light on things, I suppose. You did all this just to get your hands on this piece of paper?'' He held up a plain white eight-by-ten with typing on one side. "Just for this?''

"Jus' for this,'' Ralph answered mournfully. They all glared at him for a moment. He tried to drain two more drops out of an empty glass. At Brad's nod, Alfred refilled the glass.

Brad sighed as he folded the paper and slipped it into his inside jacket pocket. He seemed hardly to notice that he missed the pocket, and when he got up the paper fell to the floor.

"But——'' Em started to say.

"Shut up,'' Alfred spat.

"Ralph, my friends and I have to talk this thing over. Breaking and entering, Em?''

"Twenty years *in the night time*,'' Em assured him.

"Boy, that's a long time. Well, we'll talk it over and decide whether we ought to call the cops or not, Ralph. You wait right here.''

As she followed the two men out of the door into the adjoining study Em could hardly still her nerves. One quick look behind her showed Ralph vainly reaching for the paper and the brandy bottle, all at the same time.

Inside the study Brad collapsed into an overstuffed chair with a massive sigh. "Do you suppose...?" he asked Alfred.

The little man shrugged his shoulders. "He's the right type," he said. "And if we give him time to think he'll surely fall for it."

"What are you two concocting?" Em asked imperiously. "Surely you don't think that Ralph is going to——?"

"Of course he is," Brad interrupted. "He's going to look on that piece of paper as a gift from the gods. He's going to...break out of here—better make sure the lights are on in the hall and on the porch, Alfred. We wouldn't want him to fall all over himself." And then back to Emily. "And then he's going to run to his boss, and not say a word about the fouled-up so-called break-in. And then he's——"

"And then he's going to show that listing and make believe he stole the thing all by himself," Em interrupted excitedly. "Only——"

"Only the paper's a fake," Brad told her. "A complete and total fake."

Emily plumped herself down in the sofa. "Lord, what a pair of rotten schemers you two are. You make me look as pure as the driven snow. How could you be so——?"

"Devious, is the word," Brad said. "Devious. A nice, fat, round, lovable word. Alfred, you'd better get out in the hall and give our house breaker any assistance he might need."

The little man seemed indignant. "And leave you alone with——?"

"Alfred!"

"All right. I'm going. But I've warned you before. This one will break up our whole life. I warned you!"

"I know, you warned me." The little man grimaced at Emily and glided out of the door as silent as a ghost.

"Devious," Emily muttered. "Rotten and devious. How in the world could a girl fall in love with a man who is like that?"

His chair was close enough for him to move from one to the other without his crutches. "Is that what you've done, Em?" One of his arms came around her shoulders. She slumped over slightly into the comfort of him, and blinked her eyes.

"I guess—maybe I have," she whispered. "I didn't mean to. You're not a good sort of man to fall in love with, but I just can't seem to help myself. Maybe it's all the confusion this past two weeks. Your accident, Rob's appearances, the little lost girl—all that. Maybe if I go back home and get a good night's sleep, and then maybe if I took a week or so off, then maybe I could——" She was interrupted by Sheba, who came wandering in at just that moment, sat for a minute in front of both of them to appraise the situation, and then vaulted up onto the couch beside him.

"And even my cat," she added disgustedly. "*My* cat! My grandmother gave me that cat—did you know that?"

He thought it was the better part of valor to say nothing, but he did nod.

Em squirmed around so that her knees were up on the couch and she was facing him directly. "My cat," Em continued. "She never loved anyone. Well, occasionally she loved me. And you've stolen her away from me, damn you!"

"Not stolen," he said in that soft baritone voice that mesmerised her, "not stolen. Just borrowed. We're all going to be together, you and I and Sheba."

"I... don't understand." And for some stupid reason she began to cry, and couldn't find her little lace handkerchief. He tugged approximately one square foot of handkerchief from his coat pocket and passed it to her. She buried her face in the scented softness.

"You and I, Emily. We're going to get married, and Sheba is going to live with us and love us both forever and ever."

"Married? That's ridiculous."

"No. It's the only practical thing to do, my dear."

"I don't think so," she muttered. She stopped long enough to blow her nose. The last tear had fallen. "I don't see how we could get married. First of all, I may be in love with you—*may be*. But I know for darn sure I don't really *like* you. At least not all the time. There are times that you... frighten me. I don't know what to make of you sometimes. Are you really a rotten, mean-spirited fellow? That's what you wanted me to believe last week. Do you ever do good to people? Oh, I don't mean with a Christmas check, or things like that, but things that you have to *do* by yourself?"

"Rebuttal?"

"Yes." She settled back again into the warmth of his arms and looked up at him. There was no possible way he could be called handsome, she told herself. Determined, virile, hawk-eyed, in total control of himself. But never handsome. Yes, her conscience responded, and I'm not pretty. Surely God never intended that only the handsome ones fell in love and got married? She blushed at her own conclusions. "Well, were you going to say something?"

"I've changed my mind," he said. "There's nothing I can *tell* you. There's lots I could show you!"

"I don't know about that."

"How about a thirty-day consignment?" he offered.

She bit her lower lip and stared down at her own hands, folded and fidgeting in her lap. "I don't understand."

"Consignment," he explained. "You take me on for thirty days without pay or promises, and then if after that time I prove myself you get to keep me. How's that?"

"I—I don't know," she said. "Let me go."

She was instantly released, and managed to scramble to her feet and take a wobbly step or two away from him.

"Of course you understand," he said almost in a whisper. "You have to go around with me, day and night, for the thirty days, before you make up your mind."

"Go around with you?" She gasped, and a finger fled to her mouth.

"Yes. You know. Live in my house, share breakfast with me, travel around with me to see what I'm up to."

"But—but——"

"All right," he said finally. "But it's the only way, Em. Pick out two or three things that are important to you in a relationship, and try them out. I'll do the same. At the end of thirty days we'll know whether we'd be compatible."

Her breath ran out of her like a sail emptying the wind. A little color returned to her face. She unfurled her fists. Where the fingernails had dug into her palms there were little red slits.

"But not in your bed?"

"Well, not unless you want to." His big black eyes lit up in unholy glee.

"I . . . can't conceive that I'd want to," she said self-righteously.

"No, no, of course not." Was that a little sarcastic? she asked herself. Thirty days. It would give her time to really evaluate him. She was so busy thinking that she missed his additional whispered statement, "Not at first, that is."

"I...might be able to do that," she said, as primly as she knew how. "It'll give me a chance to compare you to Robert."

"Oh, hell!" he yelled at her. "You and your damn Robert. Get out of here, woman!"

Emily *got*, at high speed. Brad Colson fumbled for his crutches and made his way back to the empty kitchen. Only the brandy bottle was on view; he picked it up and drank directly from the bottle, then wiped his lips with his coat sleeve before he sat down again. Alfred came in at just that moment.

"He's gone," the little man reported. "Staggered out as if he were holding a Ming vase. I just hope he doesn't get arrested for driving drunk. Took the bait for sure."

"Yeah," Brad responded gloomily. "Wonderful planner, aren't I? So how come she turned me down?"

A broad smile coasted across Alfred's narrow face, and quickly disappeared. "Turned you down, now, did she? Well, I told you she was the marrying kind." He walked over to the bottle and toasted himself and the bachelor world.

"My gawd," Brad remarked. "Do you think she didn't know I was proposing marriage? What did I say?" He ruminated for several minutes. "I *said* marriage, as plain as day. And she turned me down. Would you believe that?"

"No, I rather think I can't believe that."

"Maybe I should have stuffed *her* with brandy as well as that house breaker. Do you think——?"

"Not a chance." Alfred looked around the kitchen. "A light repast?"

"I couldn't eat a thing. How is it possible that that little mouse of a girl could turn me in circles like this? What did I do wrong?"

"I suspect you were too pleasant to her during the first day or two," Alfred commented. "Early failures like that lead one to doomsday road every time."

"Oh, shut up, you damn grouch." Brad thumped both elbows down on the table and glared out of the window into the darkness. There was nothing to be seen, which suited his troubled mind exactly.

"So she'll be off about her business," Alfred asked cheerfully.

"Damned if that's so," Brad replied. "I talked her into a thirty-day trial period."

"A thirty-day——"

"Yes. And you'd damn well better toe the line, Mr. Sutherland, or there'll be hell to pay in these parts. You hear me?"

"I hear you," Alfred grumbled. "I think your foot must hurt you more than you think. This is entirely irrational. When are you going to take back control of the company?"

"Very soon. I've more than enough proxies to do the work."

"Then why not tomorrow?"

Brad Colson wheeled around and glared at the little man. "Don't press, Alfred. Don't press. We've seen a lot of water pass under the bridge, you and I, but that doesn't give you control over my life. I don't have much maneuver-room here. Right now I have a more important priority than that damn company."

"Women," Alfred muttered as he bustled around the room, picking up.

*   *   *

Emily managed to duck out of the hall into what had once been the library when she heard Ralph wander up out of the kitchen. He was singing softly to himself, weaving from side to side, waving a piece of white paper in his hands as though he had found the Holy Grail.

She followed him out onto the porch, and was sitting on the top stair, huddled against the banister, when his car roared into action and wobbled down Briggs Street. Only God will keep him out of the slammer tonight, she told herself as she closed her eyes and leaned back. She had only joined MADD—Mothers Against Drunk Driving—a week ago. They'll be asking for my resignation tomorrow. Damn. Bradley Colson. Time to evaluate what I know.

He's about thirty-five, a little wild on occasion, stubborn as a Missouri mule, and he thinks that I'm...sexy? Even Rob never said anything like that to me. But, for that matter, Rob never was highly romantic. He was a man who believed in sex three or four times a week, but only in bed in the dark of night. Why was that, do you suppose, Em? In the dark he didn't have to see me?

But that was nonsense. Rob was a good husband. He came home from work tired to the bone, especially when he had to work late. Nobody can turn it on all the time. Nobody, except some kind of satyr—if there really *was* such a creature. The real trouble, Em told herself, is that I haven't any experience. Four years of marriage to Rob left me with four years of knowledge about how Rob did things. Do all men go about it in the same way that Rob did? Wasn't there something else to life than a quick tumble in the hay? Surely, on occasions—rare occasions—going to bed with Rob had been very stimulating. And on most of the other nights it had been— well, warmly comforting to know that she was providing him with such a wonderful experience. But wasn't there something more?

"You need more experience, girl," she told herself. So how about Brad Colson's offer? She blushed at the thought. There was something so darn...commercial in the idea that you could make an arrangement beforehand for—Lord, it seems so coldhearted! Is that the way Brad is? Maybe there's the answer! It's a hard world, and to get hard answer a girl has to... What am I thinking? You know darn well what you're thinking of, she told herself. There's only one test for compatibility that you would want to make. Only one. Em shivered, not from the breeze, but from her own thoughts.

Maybe I could ask Rob? But that was a thought that could not fly. First of all, her psychic powers were all passive. She could be called, but could not herself call. She could feel dreams and dreamers, but could not reach out into the emptiness for them. And if Rob were truly here would she have the nerve to ask him? Sex was a subject not discussed, not in Rob's home.

She could—she could rest her head against the banister rail and empty her mind and...feel the wild penetration of a myriad troubled minds on this cold, damp night. There was love and murder and assault and robbery, all compressed into a sudden assault that spun her mind around. Usually she knew enough not to concentrate so strongly, but tonight everything collapsed in on top of her. Em Sturtevant screamed as she tumbled down the stairs. Brad Colson, his crutches almost tripping him, came rattling down the hall to help.

"Exhausted," Dr. Hastings said as he straightened up and tucked his stethoscope away in his shirt pocket. "Known her since she was two years old. Always a sensitive little thing, our Emily. Needs rest, fresh air, no badgering. Finest nurse in town, but people keep imposing on her—— Ah, she's coming around. Em, what the devil have you been up to now?"

"Telephone," she gasped. "Telephone. I need to——"

"You need to settle back in bed and cut out these shenanigans," the doctor said firmly. "Cut out all this fancy dieting. Steak and potatoes, that's what."

"I have to call the police," she managed to get out.

He held up his hand imperiously. "No calls, no movements, no stress—or I'll clap you in the psycho ward so fast it'll make your ears ring!"

"Bully." Said softly, and with affection. His eyes were twinkling as he turned away from her.

"And you, young man. You are——?"

"Colson; Bradley Colson."

"And you plan to be responsible for this tyke?"

Em lifted herself up on her elbows. It was considerable strain. "No," she objected. "He's not responsible for me. I'm going home."

"Shut up," Brad muttered as he pushed her back down in the bed.

"Wise beyond your years, young man," the doctor said.

"I can't stand the man," Em grumbled. "God knows what he'll do to me if you leave me alone with him."

"Emily, shut up!"

"And don't talk to me like that!"

"Always was a handful," Dr. Hastings commented as he closed up his bag. "Look, sonny, feed her up, keep her in bed and call me in forty-eight hours. Colson, did you say? Not the shoe Colsons? I bought a pair of shoes from you people twenty-two years ago, and they finally wore out. The new pair is terrible. You people don't make things the way you used to. Somebody ought to be horsewhipped.''

"Yes, sir," Brad said. "I'll see to it. Alfred here will help you to your car."

"No need to push," the doctor said, chuckling. "I haven't made up my bill yet. All right, I'm going!"

"Does he always run on like that?" he asked Emily. She grinned at him.

"The doctor is seventy-seven years old. *Sonny.* I liked that. Now, about the telephone?"

"You could at least wait until he gets out of the house."

"No, I couldn't." Em was all seriousness and concern. "No, time is always important. Bring me the telephone."

He hesitated for a moment, a complex man faced with a complex problem. "Another of your visions, I suppose?"

"You don't have to believe in them," she replied. "But—time is important. I see things, but I never know whether they are past, present, or future."

"Crazy," he murmured. "But if you want a girl I guess you have to take her lock, stock, and barrel. Who do you want to talk to?"

"Anybody at the police station," she said, and relaxed against the pillow as he turned on his heel and went out of the room. Why, he's really rather nice, she thought as her eyes followed his broad back. At least he's willing to understand. That's a mark in his favor. And "if you want a girl I guess you have to take her lock, stock, and barrel"? Nothing wrong with that as a place to start. And I guess I'd have to take him for the same, wouldn't I? If.

In a moment he was back again, trailing a telephone wire behind him, the instrument in his hand and at his ear. "Sergeant Mulhaley," he said. She nodded and reached up for the instrument.

"Emily," she said. "Emily Sturtevant. Yes. The little girl. She has either been, or is, or will be soon taken out of her condo and placed in a black limousine. Cadillac, I think. They'll be heading for route four-nine-five. I don't know which roads."

The voice on the other end made comforting noises, so that Em finally stopped her tears and smiled. Brad Colson shook his head as she returned the telephone to him. "I don't understand. He believes all that mummery?"

"Of course he does." She looked up at him solemnly. Her strength was returning, as if a boisterous river were refilling her reservoir. "First of all, psychic functions have been proven to be successful. Second, the police have no other leads; third, I have a record of past successes. And fourth..." She stopped long enough to finger-comb her hair; long enough to test his patience.

"And fourth, what?"

"And fourthly, Sergeant Mulhaley is my godfather."

He groaned and slowly shook his head. "Ghosts and mediums and soothsayers and things that go bump in the night," he muttered as he started out of the bedroom door to dispose of the telephone.

"You don't have to believe it all in one fell swoop," she called after him. When he was truly gone she relaxed against the pillows, suppressed a sigh, and crossed her arms tightly over her bosom to hold in the spurts of terror that always haunted her after a psychic contact. She had never met the little girl, but there was a thread of a connection that let her feel the child's pleasures and fears. There was enough of it to almost overcome the feeling of dread she had for the missing child.

"I wish I had a child," she told the lamb that gambolled on the yellow-sprigged wallpaper. *Rob and I?* No, Rob had never wanted a child. "Not yet," he'd said time after time to her pleadings. "Later."

She was too embarrassed to continue the thought in public, so she ducked her head under the sheet. *Brad and I?* It had the sound of perfection, but at the same time it was a criticism of Rob, and she was not ready for that. Not at all. She struggled with her problem, and, struggling, fell asleep.

When Brad Colson came back a few minutes later she was breathing through her mouth, almost snoring. The sheet covered half her face. He pulled it back gently and tucked it in. In repose she was a gamine darling. Not a young maiden, but a balanced woman. "And yes," he whispered to himself, "you're beautiful." With that benediction he kissed her lightly on the forehead, and went back downstairs to see what the world of business chicanery had on its so-called mind.

CHAPTER EIGHT

THREE days later Brad walked out on his front porch to find Emily sitting cozily beside a very young policeman. Brad was walking better. His doctor had traded his cast and crutches for a smaller cast and a cane. "Good morning," she offered tentatively.

"Hmp," he grumbled. "Are you supposed to be out of bed?"

"Yes. The doctor okayed it yesterday afternoon. Sergeant Hill has just told me some wonderful news."

I'll bet, he told himself. Anything to clutter up my life with these damn shiny young policemen. But what the hell——? I'm not jealous, am I?

"Yes," the policeman volunteered. "We caught the father with a roadblock just before he got on to four-nine-five. The kid was yelling like crazy."

"You mean she loved her mother more than her father?" Brad shook his head dismally.

"Not exactly," the officer chuckled. "Seems she was scheduled to play the lead in her school play, and she didn't want to have him ruin her stage chances by kidnapping her to Florida." The young man got up and resettled his pistol holster. "But we owe it all to you, Miss Emily. One more psychic victory for our side. See you." He gave Em a big smile and Brad a cold nod, all of which infuriated him.

Em turned slightly to look at him. "You weren't here yesterday."

"Is that an accusation?"

"No—I . . . don't know why I said that."

"I was at a business meeting," he told her. "Has my mother been bothering you?"

"I——" The woman is his mother, Em thought. No matter what I think of her and the way she's carrying on, she is his mother. And if I want to learn to get along with Brad then I'd better learn to get along with his mother, right? Let me think that through one more time. Quotation: I want to learn to get along with Brad! And all it implies. How can I not know that I've fallen in love, head over teakettle? And about his mother?

"Well?"

"Your mother? We've—er—only met a couple of times, you know. And most people have trouble with their——"

"Mother-in-law," he interrupted.

"I . . . think it's a little early to use a word like that, isn't it?"

"I don't think so. Everything's set, just waiting for the word from you." He paused, and looked down at her thoughtfully. And I'd better get my licks in now before some other damn policeman sweeps her off, he told himself bitterly. "Or is it something that my mother has said or done that keeps you from saying the word?"

It was hard for her to avoid his eyes—or fail to give a true answer. She fumbled for words, and found nothing to fit.

"Damn," he muttered as he reached for her hand. "Come on."

"Come on where?"

"We're going to have this out right now. We're going to get my mother playing on the right sheet of music. Up you come."

"I don't feel very well," she lied.

"You look fine."

"The doctor said——"

"That you're going to my mother's house right this minute."

"Brad!"

"Are you afraid of a little old lady?"

"If she were little I probably wouldn't be," she answered gloomily. "But she's just as big as you could want. I——"

"Get your hat."

"I don't have a hat. They're not much in style among the general public."

"Playing in circles just to keep out of range, aren't you, little witch?" There was a tender smile on his face. "A real witch. And all mine."

"Don't be ridiculous. I'm not a witch, and if I were you couldn't own me. No way!" She reached over and scratched behind Sheba's ear. Her cat purred loudly enough to be heard across the street.

"Not a witch, huh?"

"Stop it, Brad!" She jumped to her feet and glared at him. "How would you like it if people pointed you out on the streets and called you a warlock, or something? I'm just a woman who—occasionally—has visions. That's all!"

"Of course it is. I have a vision too." He held out his hands to her. Almost like a zombie, she walked into his arms and was carefully folded into his warmth.

"Look at Sheba," she whispered. "Now *she's* a real witch. She thinks something is going to happen to me. She's been camping out next to me for the past twenty-four hours, prepared to protect me."

"Well, something *is* going to happen to you," he murmured softly, and those warm lips came down on hers and swept her away from time and place to another sort of vision. She was breathing hard as he released her. "Come along with me?"

She needed no time to consider. "Yes," she said, surrendering. He tucked her under his arm and led the way out to the car. Sheba paced alongside, hissing from time to time, her torn ear standing straight up. When he opened the back door of the car the cat brushed by them both and ensconced herself on the seat.

"Bodyguard," he acknowledged as he ushered Emily into the front seat. "Crazy, that cat. Well, here we go."

And there they did indeed go. Out to route one-three-eight, and then north to the settled area between route four-nine-five and the lakes.

"Almost in the country, isn't it?" What else could she say? And then she was struck by a fine idea. She inched over in the front bench seat until her hip ran aground on his, and managed to wrap one arm around his. Loosely, of course. There was more than one way to put a car into a ditch. He freed one hand from the wheel and dropped it to her knee.

And there's another way to have an accident, she told herself as she tried to trap his wandering hand with her own. It was easy enough to catch up, but almost impossible for him to give up her knee. And so they made the rest of the trip in close, wary contact. Em loved it.

"Just a little bit further up ahead," he announced as they turned west on Field Street. And so it was. A fine gray fieldstone house, two floors and a highly peaked red slate roof, with an attached three-car garage, all full.

"Dear me," she muttered. Brad pulled over to the kerb and chuckled at her.

"Don't let it over-impress you, love. It's only a house. My father built it to hold all of us. My mother lives there alone now—not counting her cats and her birds, and any little hobbyist she's gathered in. Oh—and her five servants."

"Don't sound so cynical," she commanded. "No matter what, she's still your mother. No wonder she needs such a high monthly income. Keeping a house like this must cost her a bundle."

"I pay all the housing expenses," he snapped. "Come on, we can't sit here all day." He slid out of the car, and Sheba followed close behind. "Bring that case on the back seat," he directed.

"Yes, sure," she said under her breath. "Is this the way marriage is going to be? You great warrior, me squaw?" Reluctantly she did as she was bid, and trailed behind him to the front door.

"Madam is in the study," the very imperial butler said. "With Mr. Greystone. Shall I announce you?"

"Don't bother, Elmer," Colson snapped. "This is my wife, Emily. I know the way. Can't you go a little faster, Em? I've only got a foot and a half to work with, and you can't keep up." Em closed her mouth and breathed faster. My wife? What is this man up to?

"Yes," she said. "This darn thing is heavy and——"

"Oh, dear Lord," the butler interrupted. "Was that a cat with you? Lady Mel is loose in the house, sir."

Emily stopped to look around. The hall was dim, even though there was a glass dome two flights up, over the entrance. Sheba had disappeared.

"I wouldn't want your cat to be injured," the butler added.

"Lady Mel?" Em asked.

"My mother's cat," Brad answered. "Spoiled as the day is long."

"You don't like the cat?"

"God, no."

"Then forget it. When Sheba tracks her down they'll announce themselves."

Brad looked at her and coughed. She nodded her head. He shrugged his shoulders. "This way, love." She picked up the case and followed along behind him, whistling in the semidark.

Somehow or another the butler managed to get by them, and was standing at the closed doors of the study, which he threw open. "Mr. and Mrs. Colson," he announced in a surprisingly deep voice.

Em took a deep breath. The premature announcement of her marital status took all the wind out of her sails, so she concentrated on looking around. The study was about as big as all four of the bedrooms at her home on Briggs Street. French windows sparkled on three sides, wall to ceiling. The centerpiece of the room was a twenty-foot mahogany table, gleaming with the dull gloss of tender care. A number of papers were spread across one end of the table, where Mrs. Colson, ignoring the man beside her, glared up at them both.

"Mr. and Mrs. Colson?" She half rose from her chair and then sank down again. "Brad, you fool. You could have done a thousand times better."

"No, I know that's not true," he said as he made his way over to the table. He was tired. Em could see his fingers shaking as they grabbed the back of one of the chairs for support. "I don't think anyone in the world could match Emily's capacity for love and devotion."

"You're deceiving yourself," his mother returned. "A mother always expects more for her only son than she ever gets, I suppose."

"I suppose that's right," Brad said. "We have a——"

"And a witch to boot," his mother continued, just as if he hadn't said a word. There were tears in the old lady's eyes. For a moment Em almost felt like comforting her, but then she had a swift afterthought. I know a good many women who can cry on demand, she told herself. Including me.

"And secondhand, to boot," his mother added, immediately spoiling her initial effect.

"What are you talking about?" Brad snarled.

"Secondhand," his mother repeated sternly. "Can you deny it? Another man has had her. And Lord only knows how many others beside her first husband."

"And that is the...last damn straw," Brad roared. He pulled out the chair in front of him and sat down. "I'm bloody glad that you've got your tame accountant with you." He nodded to the other man, short, plump, and dressed entirely in gray, from his shining shoe tips to the monk's tonsure that surrounded his bald top.

"Greystone, are those the corporate summaries you have there?" Brad said. His hand reached for one of the spreadsheets. "Just what we need," he continued.

"Don't show him a thing," Mrs. Colson snapped. "He'll be voted out of office tomorrow. He doesn't have the right to inquire about the books."

"But until tomorrow..." Brad Colson said. Em, dropping into a chair beside him, shivered at the coldness of the tone. She put one placating hand on his arm. He placed his other hand on top of hers.

"But until tomorrow," the accountant said, "you...are still the——"

"Don't tell him a thing," Mrs. Colson shouted. She stood up and tried to sweep the papers away from Brad. He caught both her hands and held them.

"You were saying, Greystone?"

"Er—until tomorrow you are still the president and chief operating officer." All said with a rush, and accompanied by a shuffle as the little gray man slid another chair down the table.

"And how many proxies do you have, Greystone?"

The accountant's face turned pale. "Not enough," he mumbled.

"You fool. You stupid fool," Mrs. Colson muttered.

"But we know where they are," Greystone said apologetically. "We know exactly who is holding enough shares to give us voting control of the corporation."

Brad Colson chuckled and patted Em's hand gently. "Who might that be?" he asked gently.

"Some woman. She lives right here in Taunton," the accountant said. "I've already sent both my assistants to her. We'll pay twenty per cent higher than the board rate, and by tomorrow——"

"Why don't you tell me the name of this woman?" Brad said. His mother looked over at him suspiciously.

"Who?" she asked.

The accountant rustled through the papers at his elbow. "It seems to be a Mrs. Emily Sturtevant," he muttered. "She's been buying up small lots of shares off the market for the last fifteen days. My people can't find any record of her being in the market before this month."

Mrs. Colson seemed to be blowing up. Her face turned purple, and her already capacious bodice expanded a couple of inches. When she started to talk the breath ran out of her like a train whistle on a cold New England night.

"Why, you fool! You ever-loving double-dyed ignoramus. Why didn't you tell me earlier? Oh, God, what an absolute mess this is. Do you know who this Emily Sturtevant is?"

"I hadn't really had a chance to look into it further," Greystone stuttered. "I was completely tied up and you were unavailable until just now and..." The little man was perspiring madly as he searched vainly for a way out.

"Well, you needn't search any further," Brad Colson said gently. "This lady sitting next to me is Emily Sturtevant, and here in this case I have the additional proxies that put me back in control of Colson Enterprises."

The silence that fell over the room was momentary. Mrs. Colson seemed to be almost frothing at the mouth. Mr. Greystone was doing his best to cram all the papers he had brought with him into his own brown case.

"And I'm sorry to tell you this, Greystone," he continued gently, "but as of now you are unemployed. I would suggest you file at the unemployment bureau as soon as you can. Oh, and don't make any plans to leave the state. I've already had a talk with the district attorney about embezzlement and things like that."

"Mrs. Colson?" The little man made an appeal to Caesar, or Caesar's mother, to be exact.

"Don't worry," that worthy declared. "I am still the treasurer of the corporation. Just keep your mouth shut and I'll——"

"Oh, did I forget that?" Brad drawled. "All of this is too much for a lady of your age, mother. As of tomorrow morning you are officially retired. There'll be a small pension, of course."

Mrs. Colson had been defeated, but not destroyed. Em could see the anger rising behind those dark eyes. "But I can't possibly keep up the house on anything less than what I'm making," she pleaded.

"No, you surely couldn't," he agreed. "But you don't have to worry about that. The house, you'll remember, belongs to me. I'm not sure that we would want to live here ourselves, but you can be positive that you *won't* be living here—without Emily's prior approval. And, just to give yourself a small taste of what's to come, I suggest you pack and leave this afternoon. The summer house down on the Cape will be available to you until Emily comes to some conclusion."

"Damn you," the matriarch muttered. "Damn you. I should have had you drowned when you were born! Get out of here, Greystone." The little man grappled for his briefcase.

"No, just leave the papers there," Brad told him. "You can use your company car until tomorrow noon." Greystone scurried away. Elmer, the butler, appeared at the door looking a question.

"See that Mr. Greystone gets safely off the premises," Brad directed. "And then have someone pick up all these papers and lock them up in the safe. And, while you're at it, have someone help my mother to pack. She'll be leaving also."

"Damn you. Damn you!" Mrs. Colson screamed. "It's all your fault, you damn witch. I'm going to..."

She started around the table in Emily's direction, but hardly gained her objective. A startling scream echoed off the rafters, the butler was knocked off his feet, and a purebred Persian cat came squalling into the room, vaulted up onto the table, and slid halfway down into Mrs. Colson's protective arms. She was a large cat, some fifteen pounds or more, but all her fire had gone. Her legs were still scrambling into her mistress's chubby arms, claws out, when Sheba came stalking in through the door.

"What have you done?" Emily asked, shocked. Her cat, as usual, paid her no attention, but looked around for a second, then vaulted up on the table and began stalking her prey.

"Sheba. Sit!" Brad Colson, in his magnificent commanding voice. And Sheba sat.

"Well, I'll be——" Em started, and then refurbished her language. Both of them, man and cat, had completely startled her. Sheba stretched out and began to clean up her claws. Mrs. Colson, completely at sea, fell back into one of the big chairs, her cat hung around her neck like a fur piece.

"I do believe that Lady Mel attacked the—er—visitor," Elmer commented.

"Perhaps you could get one of the maids to help my mother to her room. And her cat as well?" Brad said.

"I...yes," the butler said. "Providing someone could control that attack-cat?" He did something behind his back, and a bell rang faintly in the distance.

Brad reached over and picked Sheba up, cuddling her against his shoulder.

"You...how did you do that?" Em muttered.

"Psychology," he said, chuckling. "Just a demonstration, my dear. I mean to be the ruler in my little family."

"Is that some sort of a hint?" she asked, and then as Mrs. Colson was led by her, "Can I help you at all, ma'am?"

"Don't come near me. And don't call me ma'am. God, a witch in the family. I can't believe it."

"Believe it," her son called after her as the butler ushered her out of the study and closed the door behind them. There was finally silence in the study, until Sheba sounded off. Em checked her watch. It was time for the cat's daily feeding.

"Finished, have you?" she asked Brad. He looked up at the strain in her voice.

"Almost," he sighed. "Obviously you don't like the way things happened."

"And that's stating it simply," she returned. "You've been using me, all this time. Using my name to buy up shares in your corporation, using me for a mask to deceive your mother—all that bit about bugging, and burglarizing . . . all that was just a come-on, to keep your mother, and me too, for that matter, completely in the dark!''

"Something like that," he agreed as he walked around the end of the table and put an arm on her shoulder. "But not entirely."

She shook his arm off. "No, not entirely," she muttered. "I suppose there are plans within plans within plans? And how could you treat your mother like that? You know darn well I'd never displace her from her home. Your own mother! You've got a heart like a piece of ice, Brad Colson!''

"Yes, I think I could plead guilty to all that," he said. "But you don't know what it's been, Em—all these years living with my family. I think my father died happy."

"What are you saying?" Her flushed face was being scoured with tiny tears as her mascara began to run.

"I'm saying that I think my father was glad to die, rather than be haunted forever by my mother! He was a . . . gentle man. Can you understand that?''

"I'm afraid it's all beyond me," she said as she automatically took the handkerchief he extended. "I'm a simple sort of person." Another dab or two. "And you lied. You told them we were already married, and we aren't, and——"

"Not that too," he protested.

"Look at me," she snapped. "In all the time I've known you you've taught me to lie and steal and cheat, and I feel as if I——" The water gates opened again as tears streamed down her face. Sobbing, breaking tears, until he pulled her to her feet and held her close in his comforting arms.

"I still have you, Em, don't I?"

It was a question she had not anticipated. *Do I still have you?* Did it matter, all these things he had done? Must a man be perfect in all persuasions in order for one to love him? Her mother had told her before she'd married Rob that a girl should never marry a man intending to reform him. You have to take him as he comes. And yet...?

"Don't count on it," Emily told him. "You used me. Without even asking, you used me."

He turned to her, a grieving look on his face, and for once he fumbled for words. "I didn't use *you*," he said. "I used your name to buy a few shares of stock. There's a difference. The law requires that purchases be made in some real name. I thought I was doing you an honor by using your name. In fact, the shares are yours. I always intended that my wife would share in the leadership!"

"I suppose if I had a college degree," she said, "I might be able to discern the subtle difference in your twisted logic. But I don't have the education. I guess my sights were set too high."

"How so?"

Hug me, her mind shouted at him. Don't stand there with your hands in your pockets, debating. Hold me. You can't convince me by words! But he was not receiving the message.

"I guess it's the foolish dream of every young widow," she said, shrugging her shoulders in disgust. "You wouldn't know. The dream that, having had a perfect husband and lost him——"

"Perfect?"

Em stepped back from him. He looked fierce enough to do her some bodily harm, and she still did not know why.

"Yes, perfect. Rob was...everything. And like sóme dewy little innocent I expected to—that I would find another man just as perfect. Stupid, I know. But Rob was romantic perfection. And you——"

"Yes? Me what?"

"I know it's not your fault," she replied. "But there you are, warts and all. And I guess——"

"You guess what?"

"I don't know, do I? I would appreciate it, Mr. Colson, if you would take me home. And would you please get all those shares of stock transferred out of my name? I don't even know the game we're playing, but I want out."

"Whatever you wish," he said gloomily.

"Immediately."

"Yes."

The trip back to Briggs Street was made in high-speed silence. Emily relaxed in the comfort of his upholstered car seats, and did her best not to look at him. To her surprise Sheba had climbed into the car and coiled up in her lap. And throughout the trip her mind poked and prodded at her problem.

Warts and all. What a silly phrase. He hadn't a wart to his name. Well, not anywhere that she could see. And of course he was not as romantic as Rob; but he was a solid citizen nonetheless. The sort of man you could count on in a melee. No, he wasn't handsome, but then the world was not overly full of handsome men.

And there was something else. She had been totally dependent on Rob for her living. Before she was finally capped she had earned hardly as much as the boy on the paper round. Now she was a senior nurse, could command a good salary, and had no real need for a man in her life.

No need? Then why did her very bones ache to have him, to be with him, to——? Why? And at that point he pulled up in front of the house on Briggs Street, set the parking brake, loosened his seat belt and turned in her direction.

"Well, Miss Emily, would it do any good to apologize?"

"Not hardly," she sighed.

"Then I suppose you're about to give me my walking papers?"

"I...not necessarily, Bradley. A girl can hardly expect perfection on the second time around. Give me a chance to think this thing through?"

He settled back in his seat, and seemed to emit a massive sigh. "Well," he said as he climbed out of the car, "what a nice day it is." Deep silence. "Sheba, *you* certainly think it's a nice day."

Her cat stirred in her lap, stretched, walked over to and out of the driver's door, and headed down the hill towards her playground, the barn. He shook his head. "I'm a born loser," he muttered.

Em was not able to resist. He *was* a nice enough man, although not exactly the gold ring on the merry-go-round. And her heart went out to him. "My cat and I do not necessarily think the same way," she told him. "In fact, hardly ever."

She climbed out of the car and made her way into the house. Although she just could not turn around to look, it *did* sound as if the man behind her was whistling.

The day passed quietly. The "underground" corporate offices downstairs seemed to be slowly disbanding. Emily kept out of the way, not even joining him for lunch or dinner. She was wrestling with her conscience, and conscience was winning. "So two out of three and I'm a loser," she told her mirror. "Let's try for three out of five? Or five out of seven?"

Her argument went on until she looked up and found suddenly that it was dusk and she was out on the porch of his house in a gathering wind. A true storm was forming, the first one of winter. Emily shuddered and wrapped her arms around herself. Winter was a disease, according to her theories of the world. Winter was a time when God ran out of sunshine, and had to use snow to cover up Her deficit. Winter was a time to be enjoyed—when viewed through a thermopane window, inside with a cozy fire.

She took one more look at the gathering clouds and made a dash for the door. Alfred was alone in the kitchen, puttering. She hadn't seen him all day. The radiators were clanking and bubbling.

"Happy winter, Alfred."

The little man looked up at her and shook his head. "By this time every winter Mr. Colson and I would be well on our way to a Caribbean island. Or occasionally to the Mediterranean." All said mournfully. The unstated case could be heard: "And if it were not for you we would be well on our way by now!" She acknowledged his hit with a little grin.

"Did you know that Brad—er—Mr. Colson won back control of his corporation today? With my help?"

"Do you say so, madam?"

It was no use, this trying to tease the little man. He had locked on his poker face, and nothing would make him change. "Darn you, Alfred. Don't call me madam. Sometimes you make me so mad I could up and marry Brad just to make you feel bad!"   .

"Please, madam. I have just eaten. I have a very sensitive stomach, what with all the changes *we* have to endure." The *royal* we, of course. Nothing less would do. But the devil was riding Emily's shoulder.

"It could happen, you know. Mr. Colson and I might possibly marry. If we did there'd be children and animals and toys—and females—around the house. Think you could stand that, Alfred?"

"One would only pray, madam, that God would be more compassionate."

She dimpled a smile at him. "Oh, She will be, She will be. Where *is* Mr. Colson?"

"Mr. Colson has retired."

Em did a most unladylike thing. She stuck her tongue out at him, and ran for the stairs. Sheba was waiting for her at the top landing. She bent down to pet her pet, and the cat allowed the affection. Seemed to crave it, for that matter. It had been a most unusual day; it might become a most memorable night.

Brad Colson slept in the large bedroom at the far end of the hall. The doors were not quite closed, and she could see the light from a low-wattage bulb. And now, she told herself, I have only to get up my courage. And then we'll see what happens about compatibility!

But saying you must get up your courage, and actually doing so, was a horse of a different color indeed. She went into her own bedroom, perched on the old-fashioned window seat, and tried out a dozen or more opening gambits. Like, "Oh, excuse me, is this *your* bedroom?" Or, "I've had a vision, Brad, about you and me." Or perhaps something more abrupt, like, "Move over, for goodness' sake." None of them seemed to be quite the thing.

So instead she gathered up nightgown and robe, and went down the hall to the only bathroom on the first floor. The supply of hot water was almost inexhaustible.

She filled the claw-foot tub almost to the brim, scattered a handful of her own bath salts, and plunged in.

Instant parboiling gave way to soothing warmth. Em lay back in the oversize tub and tried to relax. The little portable whirlpool device attached to the tub responded at the touch of the button. Warm water swelled around her, splashed over at the foot, and then settled into a delightful circulation.

And still she had come to no conclusion. The water grew cold. She drained it off and started afresh. The whirlpool again, this time forcing water in small circles around her breasts. Em made a little inspection, something she had done nightly when Rob was alive, but not lately. Everything was in place. While not overdeveloped, she had been assured many a time by Rob that she had plenty of what was required. She settled back in the tub again, spreading the Irish Spring soap liberally across her stomach and environs. Time passed, the water cooled, and she could hear the old grandfather clock downstairs strike ten. Not too early? Not too late? Suppose he's already asleep? Then what? Rob had hated to be surprised. One made an appointment with him, at least by dinnertime. And Brad? Surely he was so much different that a less formal procedure might be possible? After all, the only thing she wanted was a . . . well, a test for compatibility. On her first wedding night she had known everything there was to know about the theory, and not a single idea about the practice. And now, some years later, she wasn't sure that the same situation still didn't prevail. It was easy enough to take a book off the shelf and review the theory, but how in the devil could you recall the practice?

She shook her head wearily, and climbed out of the tub. The only answer, of course, was to go ahead and try it out! But just wait a minute, her inner voice commanded. This is wrong. You can't just run down the hall to some man and——

"Oh, shut up," Em demanded. "We have to find out if we're compatible, right? Where do man and wife require the most compatibility? In bed, of course. We'll be spending one quarter of every day in bed. One quarter of our remaining days. And if this marriage doesn't play in the bedroom then it won't play at all!" And, with her mind committed, she went ahead.

She dried herself carefully, powdered extensively, and even added a touch of Mistique to her pulse points. There was no full-length mirror in the bathroom. She squirmed around and inspected to the best of her ability.

The nightgown was silk; soft, sheer, diaphanous silk. The sort, some of her women friends said, that you would want to leave over a chair, just in case there was a fire some night! She had bought it as a wedding gift for her friend Sarah, and then hadn't had the nerve to give it to her. She ducked her head into the yoke and stood entranced as it floated down about her, clinging from time to time, drifting like a winter fall of nothing. And then her hair. She unpinned it, brushed it madly, and let it fall where it would. She grinned at herself in the small mirror. With hair she was an experienced lady. Rob had liked it long. Only if you weren't careful, after all the excitement was over, he would turn over on his side and six chances out of ten would pin her long hair under himself, setting her up for a night of tethered pain.

And when she was finished she stood in front of that same mirror and shivered. Was it a right thing to do? On a thirty-day consignment? C'mon, Emily, she finally demanded, get a wiggle on. You're running an experiment. If it works, well—and, if it doesn't, you've only wasted a couple of hours. Something teased the back of her mind, and she giggled. A couple of hours, in her experience? More than likely fifteen minutes at most. Chin up, girl; shoulders back; hup, two, three, four.

And there in front of her were the double doors. The little light still glimmered through the opening. Emily cleared her throat nervously, gave her gown a little twitch so that it might lie closely in all the proper places, and then opened the door and went in.

Brad Colson was stretched out in the middle of the queen-size bed, wearing . . . practically nothing, holding a paperback book in his hand. He heard her come in, and set the book down on the blankets. "Well," he said.

Emily took a deep breath, and promptly forgot all the phrases she had practiced. "I've come," she said hoarsely.

"Yes, I can see that." He ran one hand through his coal black hair and patted the bed beside him. "One wonders to what purpose you've come." At that one moment Emily hated him, and wished she hadn't come at all, but her feet refused her orders to run. Instead they carried her over to the bedside.

"I—came," she said, thankful that the dim light hid the blushes that flashed over most of her body. "Oh, my God, what am I doing?"

CHAPTER NINE

BRAD wasn't reacting properly. Emily looked down at herself. The light was dim, but it outlined her figure as if the nightgown were not there. He should have been startled, or staring, or even salivating. Instead he pulled himself up against the fluffed pillows, clasped his hands behind his head, and looked at her as if waiting for the next act.

"I—you said," she stuttered, "that we ought to...ought to. Compatibility. So I thought that this would be a...nice time to find out."

"Oh, I agree." His deep male voice coming out of the darkness sent a shiver up her spine. Sex was the male domain, she knew from experience with Rob, but this man just wasn't making a move. Maybe I need to get closer? she thought. Or maybe he's too tired already? Was that why he went to bed early? Am I doing something wrong?

"If...you're too tired...? Perhaps I should come another night?"

"No, no." She could almost swear there was laughter in his voice. She was proposing serious business here, and there was no place for frivolity. "No," he repeated, "this is a fine night for it." And still he did nothing. Nothing but grin, that was.

Em stiffened. So either give up the game, she told herself, or go the rest of the way! And, having come this far, Emily, you'd better go on. By tomorrow night you wouldn't have the nerve to try again!

She took two steps forward, bringing her to the foot of the old four-poster bed. This is the point, she said to herself, where you slip out of the sleeves of your nightgown and let it flutter to the floor. It was to have been the easiest part of the drill—except that she had forgotten a vital point. Her gown was the pull-over type. And there's no way a woman can get out of a thing like this without some bending over and lifting and pulling—and making a mess of my nicely combed hair! Her blush ran from the tips of her toes up to the scalp line.

"I have to put out the light," she murmured, and moved forward toward the night table.

"No." Nothing more, just the one word.

Stunned, Emily began to wonder where she had gone wrong. Rob never would do it with the light on. "No?"

"No. I like to see what I'm getting into."

Of course, she told herself. Men *must* have a variety of modes. Not every man would react as Rob would. Well, not for the little sideline parts, anyway. And here I am, a grown woman, a trained nurse, who knows all about—— And there she came to a stop. She knew all the *theory* of sex, and whatever practical aspect Rob could teach her. I'll bet there's more to learn! she told herself. So she left the lamp on, and, wiggling as best she could without being possibly indecent about it, managed to get the nightgown over her head, and let it float to the floor. He didn't say anything—or in fact do anything—but somebody in the room hissed in surprise. And it wasn't me, Em thought defensively. See, he's not dead and ready to be buried. There is some life in him! She took a deep breath, automatically elevating her full, firm breasts.

"All right," he said quietly, "if you keep holding your breath you'll eventually choke. Besides, I'm totally impressed already." He threw back the covers on the side nearest to her, and patted the sheets.

Move slowly, Em told herself. Gracefully. This isn't like Saturday night in the emergency room. The old springs groaned as they accepted her one hundred and ten pounds. She paused long enough to kick off her slippers, and then swung her feet up and pulled the covers over her. Out of the corner of her eye she watched him. He hadn't stirred a muscle, not a muscle! Gently she lowered her head to the pillow and straightened herself out on her back. Another squirm or two were required to make her fully comfortable.

"All right, I'm ready," she announced.

"You're ready?" He was having trouble breathing. In fact he almost choked himself. Em turned her head in his direction.

"You're not ready?" she asked. "What is it? Am I being too bold? If you'd rather not I could just as well wait until the weekend."

"Oh, no," he returned. He seemed to be using his knuckles to clear tears from his eyes. "Oh, no. The weekend will be too far away."

"Well, then, I'm ready," she repeated.

"Yes, so you said." A moment of silence as he tried to control his voice. "Em, you've done this sort of thing before?"

She frowned at him. "Do I need to submit a résumé? After all, I was married for four years."

"I hate to ask," he murmured, and now she knew definitely that there was a chuckle behind it all, "but is this the way you and Rob...?"

"Of course."

"And you did it quite often?"

"Well, in the first two weeks it was...often. Yes. Sometimes once every night. Later on it was—well, less than that. Is there something wrong? I really don't want to talk about Rob. In fact, I don't remember having to do much talking at all at this stage."

"No, everything's all right so far," he answered cautiously. "It's just I wouldn't want to get it wrong, you know."

And isn't that a surprise? Em thought. He's really a sensitive man.

"Just one more question, Emily."

"Yes?"

"Now that you're completely ready, what do you expect *me* to do?"

"Good Lord! Don't you know anything? I expect you to roll over on top of me, and—er—do that thing, and then . . . well, you know."

"Take about ten minutes? And you'll lie there with your eyes closed, and think of England?"

Em's eyes snapped open. "About that long, yes. And think of *England*?"

"Just an old joke," he hastened to assure her. "Well, if you're really ready?"

"I'm ready," she sighed. "It'll take a lot longer if you keep procrastinating."

"Yes, I can see that." Em adjusted herself again, flat on her back, and closed her eyes. *And think of England?* Why was he laughing?

He finally moved. One hand came over and rested on her shoulder. One large, warm hand. It moved up, and his fingers did some sort of dance on their way over to her neck. The other hand appeared, flat on her stomach. She was startled, and drew in her breath.

The hand at her neck moved up into the fringe of her hair and toyed with the lobe of her ear. She could feel the mattress shift as he turned on his side. The hand resting on her stomach began to trace little circles around her navel. Strange feelings stirred in the depths of her being. His weight shifted again. Em gave up guessing, and opened her eyes. His head blocked all her view. His lips came down gently on hers, brushed them for a moment, and then moved on.

"You don't have to be so gentle," she murmured. "I'm a very sturdy woman."

"Em," he said, "shut up. Nobody wants a gabby woman at this stage of the game."

There didn't seem to be anything else to say. Besides, she was becoming just a little bit confused. His hand had left her navel, marched smartly uphill, and came to rest, cupping her breast. She shivered in anticipation. This has to be what they call foreplay, she thought. Rob thought it was a bunch of foolishness.

His shadowed head moved. He was nuzzling her breast. The weight of his head was a nice novelty. Where am I getting all these nice new ideas? His tongue gently stroked her nipple, and then his teeth nipped at her. Her gasp was purely involuntary.

"What——?" she stammered.

"Shut up, Emily."

Yes, she told herself, shut up. He was nursing at one breast, and his hand was fondling the other. Things were no longer "nice." Things had become volcanic. Not knowing what else to do, Em managed a grip on the mattress, and held on for dear life. She could feel her breasts swelling, her nipples erect, all straining as if trying to break out of her skin's containment. And then he stopped.

"That's the end?" she asked forlornly. "Now you're going to do it?"

"Shut up, Em." But it was said in a kindly fashion. She renewed her grip on the mattress.

His lips were back on hers, resting there, waiting like a cat outside the mouse hole. She started to say something. He seized on the opening of her lips; his tongue entered and swept deliciously across to meet her own. A spark bit at her. Em shuddered.

The moan was completely unintentional. It even startled Em. He changed positions again, back down to her breast. But his hand had moved south, down across the slight swelling of her belly, off into the depths of her groin, down into the shadows. A finger probed; he was searching. And found the target. That one tiny spot which was the core and center of all her sexual reactions. He found it, touched it lightly, and the top of Em's skull came off and went flying away. He chuckled, abandoning her breast for the moment.

"This is no time to be funny," she moaned. Both her hands came up and cupped his head, leading it back to its feast. He attacked energetically, not only with his lips but with that vagrant finger torturing her almost beyond endurance. "Oh, my God," she moaned. It seemed impossible to lie still. Her legs ached with tension; the teasing went on.

For England? Em's mind, running wildly in turmoil, touched on years of variance. She wrapped her arms around his massive back, caressing the taut, smooth skin. But she wanted to do more. She squirmed and pushed and wiggled until he moved to free her. But she wanted to be free for only a moment. She rolled over on top of him, her little hands finding a perch around his waist. She pushed her way through the black curls on his chest and kissed his nipples. He smelled of soap and perspiration and maleness. And the further down she explored the more agitated he became. There, she told herself frantically, he can be influenced! But he was not about to let her have a free ride. His fingers were back, torturing her. One hand was at her breast, kneading now, with less gentleness, and more effect; the other cupped the back of her neck.

Warily she slid down lower, until her chin landed on his navel. She kissed it, treasured it. Her hand came down off the flatness of his stomach. Just a touch and he groaned. Just a touch, and Em felt the smash of lightning, the primitive urge, and withdrew. She had forgotten that men came in different sizes. And now, not knowing what or why, she wanted something more. "Do it, Brad," she muttered. "Do it now!"

He turned her over on her back, changed position, and poised himself between her legs. Without thinking, she wrapped her legs around him. She could feel the tantalizing touch of him as he swayed gently back and forth. Her head was unable to contain all the messages her nerves were sending her. But it was not teasing that she wanted. Her hands flailed desperately, trying to squeeze between his body and her own with no success. Moaning, she managed to find a handhold on the solid curve of his buttocks.

He groaned as if she had touched him in all his sensitive spots, and then he pushed gently into her. Em moaned. It had been so long ago that she almost felt like a virgin again. Another moan, and he pushed further, another inch or two. It was only a tiny movement, but it sent riotous urges up and down her spine. Her juices flooded in on him. She arched her back to hurry him on, and suddenly he posed like a diver on the high board, tested, and dived into her to his furthest capacity.

"Oh, God," she screamed. "Do it." The words came frantically as she tugged at him with all her strength, wound her legs tighter around him, bit at the shoulder that presented itself, flailed at his back with frenzied hands. He stroked gradually, and with each movement she could see stars tumble, storms blow. Up and up he took her. She tried valiantly to match his rhythm. Until finally, when she had reached a harmonious beat with him, he took her up to the edge of the clouds, up to where there was no further *up* to be found.

"Now," he muttered in her ear as his arms slipped down and he cradled the half-moons of her buttocks in his wide, capable hands. He mustered his strength, pulled her to him at the same moment that he pushed, and the world exploded.

It was many a minute before Em regained control of her errant mind, and further minutes before her body responded to command. He had led her to jump off the cloud, and she dived toward the earth in free-form floating style. The vivid colors faded, and became pastels, and she was conscious now of his head resting on the pillow beside her, his lungs pumping for air, the perspiration running down both of them. Oddly enough there were parallel scratches down his back, all oozing blood. He started to move away from her; she locked on to him and held him in place as the minutes ticked by.

"I've never——" she started to say, awed by all that had happened.

"I suspected you might never have," he said as he lifted himself up on one elbow and studied her face. "That's the best I can do for the moment, Em. I'd be a lot better after I get this damn cast off my foot." He leaned over to the end table, found a tissue, and gently wiped her forehead and her tender, aching breasts.

She thought that one over. If this is just a mediocre performance, what is there left for the big show? Oh, Robert. You knew, but you never wanted me to know!

"There are women who hardly ever achieve an orgasm," he said.

"I... never have before," she admitted. He started to roll off her, but she stopped him again. "Stay," she pleaded. "It was so wonderful! Do you suppose it could happen again?"

"Well, not right this minute," he admitted. "It takes a little... rest and refurbishment. You never... with Robert?"

"Never. Oh, it was comfortable, enjoyable, and it was my duty to help him to climax, and all that made me feel good. But never like this. God help me, never like this!"

"So—Robert was never quite perfect?"

She stirred uneasily. This new world she had found was wonderful, but she was not yet ready to criticize Rob. She tried to explain it to him. About two minutes into her explanation his hand dropped over her mouth to silence her, and he rolled off.

"You're on edge, Brad? I didn't please you?"

"You gave a stellar performance," he said, chuckling. He reached over and patted her heaving flank. "First class, Em. But we really have a problem."

"We do? I... had thought that we passed our compatibility test. That we could...go on together and get— you did mean marriage, Brad?"

"I meant marriage. I still do. But your little test has brought up a major difficulty."

"Not me. Not you?"

"Exactly. Who does that leave?"

"Well, I don't know, do I? Are you worried about this psychic material that seems to affect me from time to time? I swear I won't let it come between us, Brad. It never came between Rob and me."

"Exactly. Em, do you ever listen to yourself while you're just making conversation? Do you ever realize that, as far as you're concerned, Rob isn't really dead?"

"Why... why..." She sat up in bed, neglecting the fall of the blankets that bared her firm but aching breasts. "Why, that's a cruel thing to say," she muttered. "I *know* that Rob is dead."

"Yet he was right here in this room not a half hour ago, Em. How much of the past hour have you spent comparing me with Rob?"

"I—not as much as you might think," she murmured. "After the first two or three minutes you drove him right out of my head."

"Well, I'm pleased to hear that," he said, "but it doesn't alter the thesis. You and I are never going to find happiness, Em, so long as you continue to think of Rob as your white knight. He wasn't, you know."

She could see the spark of anger in his dark eyes. She shivered at the violence inherent in them.

"Well, he was my husband, Brad."

"Emily, I want you to do something that's going to be very painful. I want you to listen to me all the way through, no matter what. Can you do that?"

"I—suppose I could. Must I?"

"You must. Ready?"

"I'm ready," she said, and even the wind rattling the window could tell she was lying. She was *not* ready. She never ever *would* be ready. Brad looked down at her and wished he didn't have to proceed. But he knew just as well as God made little green apples that he would have to exorcise this ghost of hers.

"Em, you were working, and Rob was working. Now, where did the money go? How did you divide it all up?"

"Oh, that's easy. We used my salary for living expenses. Rob didn't like the neighborhood out here, and wanted us to have a new place over by the lake. So we lived on what I made, and he banked all of his salary for the purchase of a new house for us. Isn't that something strange to be talking about after we——?"

"Probably," he groaned. "But Em, I've had an investigator——"

"You had Rob investigated? How could you do that?"

"You said you would listen, Em."

A deep silence. She moved an inch or two, readjusting the pillow behind her head. "All right, I agreed. So you had Rob investigated. So what?"

"So how come, after all those months of saving, your former husband only had fifty-eight dollars in your joint bank account?"

"Fifty-eight dollars? I just don't know. Maybe he had some bad investments. He never talked to me about money, you know. He handled it all."

"I'm sure he did, Em. By the way, the records down at Colson Enterprises indicated that your Rob had used over one hundred and eight sick days in his last year. Now what about that?"

"Now I know somebody's lying. Rob never had a sick day in all our married life. Not one day!"

"And he was faithful forever?" There was no misconstruing the sarcasm now. It bit at her.

"Of course," she said indignantly. "None of these open marriages for us. Rob and I were a team. We were close. We had no secrets between us."

"I'm glad to hear that," he said. "Then you knew all about the apartment he maintained over on Main Street. Two rooms and a bath. The landlady said he paid regularly, but only used the place a few nights a week, he and his wife. A young wife, too."

"What? What are you trying to do to me, Brad? That wasn't Rob. It couldn't have been Rob. Not a chance in the world was that—— Why are you telling me all these lies?"

"Because you can't continue living in your little dreamworld forever, Em. Somehow I've got to get you back into the real world."

"Why?" she screamed at him. "Why?"

"Because that's where I live, Em, and if we're going to live together it has to be out here where I live. Take a look at this picture."

He passed her a glossy black-and-white picture, blown up to an eight-by-ten print. "Do you know either of these people?"

"I don't—— Why, of course, that's Rob. I've just never seen him dressed up so. I don't know the girl. Who is she?"

"Her name's Marcia," he said, cringing against the words that had to follow. "She lived in the Main Street apartment; shared it, in fact, with Rob."

The sound of the slap echoed and echoed throughout the room. I deserve that, he told himself. There has to be a better way to make the point, but I don't have the diplomacy. And now little Em was standing by the bed in her altogether, rose red from top to bottom, and ready to spit like a—like her cat.

"I don't know why you make these things up," she said slowly. "None of it's true. Rob loved me—and was faithful to me until he died."

"Was he?" Brad opened the drawer of the night table and took out another little packet of pictures. "Look at these, Em."

She hesitated and would have drawn her hand back, but he forced her to hold them, and then coaxed her to look.

"Oh, my Lord!" she exclaimed. "They look so——"

"They look so dead," he hammered at her. "Rob, and the girl that you don't know. These pictures were taken down at the morgue. Her name was Marcia Lariviere. She was only nineteen years old. She was in that car that your husband drove off the road and into the river. They died together." He had started off in almost a whisper, but as he talked his voice became louder, fiercer, as if he had a private grudge to settle. "They died together in that car, Em, your husband and little Marcia. The girl was only nineteen years old, and almost five months pregnant!"

"No!" Em released her fingers and watched the pictures fall to the floor. "I don't know why you're doing all this, Brad Colson. All the lies you've invented, all the calumny you're trying to spread about Rob—and this little girl, whoever she was. But it won't work. You're insanely jealous! And I'm glad we did this compatibility exercise, because now I know I could never marry you. We're not compatible. I'll never marry you!"

Em started for the door, then came back for her nightgown. She refused to cry. Crying was for children, not for adults! She turned on her heel, barefoot, and almost tripped over the fold in the rug. But she managed to restore her balance, and stormed out of his room, slamming the door behind her. She cried all the way down the corridor, and through the half hour it took her to pack. Sheba was almost at the point of refusing to go with her, but relented in the end. They stalked down the hill together, slammed their way into the old house at the bottom—where Emily Sturtevant fell face down on the old sofa and cried until morning.

And neither cat nor girl noticed the man standing on the porch of the house on top of the hill, cursing himself for his clumsiness. When Alfred came out to him at two in the morning he cursed the little man, fired him on the spot, and stumbled back upstairs—not to his room, but to the one that had been hers. And for the rest of the night he stood by her bedroom window, running her little scarf through his fingers as he stared out into the black of night. The scarf was all she had left behind her.

CHAPTER TEN

EMILY STURTEVANT—née Sullivan—came out onto her porch to rest. She had, for almost the past week, suffered a severe attack of guilty conscience, for which a massive dose of housecleaning was the only cure. Not a spot of room in the old house displayed a speck of dirt or dust. Even Sheba had deserted, moving herself out, bag and baggage, to the barn.

Emily had considered the barn for inclusion in the program too, but after much thought decided it might be better to burn the dilapidated old building to the ground. In any event, the bad weather of the past few weeks had fled, and for a few quiet days October was almost September. Almost. Em took herself out to the front porch to consider the world and all its troubles.

For four days she had heard not a word from the house on the hill. Oh, there had been the usual banging and swearing and loud radio playing, but no communication. And then, on the fifth day, Alfred came by. He was carrying his packed suitcase with him.

"Felt I had to stop by, Miss Emily," the little man said. "The week has only four days, and he's already fired me five times."

"Oh, Alfred, that's terrible. What will you do?"

"What I always do," he said. "I'm going down to Florida for my vacation. The bangtails are——"

"The what?" she interrupted him.

The little man shook his head, and smiled. "It's hard to believe, Miss Emily, that there could be a woman as naive as you in this harsh, bitter world. And you've done me in. Sweetness conquers villainy, three sets to one. Nags. Fillies, we call them in the old country. Here in America you call them bangtails. I don't know why. Racehorses.'' He sighed valiantly and shook his head. ''It may take us years to restore the language.''

''Ah. I may have heard the word before. I'm sorry if I've caused you any harm, Alfred. I never meant to, neither for you *nor* for Mr. Colson.''

''I know that, lady,'' he returned. ''It was always evident. He knows it too, only he's as stubborn as a donkey. One of these days it will come to him that he's wrong——''

''You don't understand, Alfred. He isn't wrong. I am. He told me certain unpalatable truths about myself and my life, and I blew up. Now that I've had a chance to think it over, all the little pieces fit into the puzzle, and he's right. Look at the new sign for my mailbox.''

''Emily Sullivan? What happened to——? Ah, I see, madam. We are——''

''We are reverting to our maiden name,'' she admitted. ''It's like shedding an old snakeskin. I can't hardly believe how much of a villain my husband was. And you're right, I'm naive—where men are concerned. Rob told me my world was full of diamonds, and they all turned out to be glass.''

''Well, if I may be so bold, Miss Emily, Mr. Colson needs you. His rotten temper has descended to the nether regions. Why don't you just go up and tell him all about your change of heart?''

''Me? Why, I'm over a hundred yards away, and already he's throwing things, right and left. He must have smashed a ton of dishes, and——''

''Only the second best,'' Alfred said. ''I—er—took the liberty of hiding the better materials in the upstairs closet. And, besides, you should know, although he throws a lot of things, he very seldom hits anything.''

''You're sure?''

''Years of experience, madam. Word on it. Do give it a good bash. I'll be back in three weeks at the outside, and nothing would make me happier than to serve the pair of you.''

''Alfred, you're sweet!''

''I certainly am not, madam,'' the little man said as he whipped out a handkerchief and wiped the spot on his forehead where she had just planted an enthusiastic kiss. ''But perhaps madam might be willing to entertain some small limit on the number of children?''

Em grinned from ear to ear. ''Believe me, if the question ever gets to the front burner, you may be sure I shall consult.''

The little man grinned again, tipped his bowler hat, and headed out to the road, where a cab had been waiting all this time.

''And the first boy's middle name shall be Alfred,'' she called after him.

''Well, really,'' she heard him say as he climbed into the waiting cab, ''one has no need to be offensive about it.'' The cab spurted away.

Em sat down again, and began to recapitulate. Rob had been a scoundrel; Brad was a darling—a stubborn, opinionated darling, who might not even know that he had been ''spoken for.'' That had to be remedied.

Rob. It could not be true that he haunted the house. More than likely I knew a great deal more about him all this time, but the knowledge was out on the periphery of my understanding, and so my oversensitive mind made a ghost out of him. Tonight—or some time soon—I must put that theory to the test.

And now, what about Brad? The longer I let him run loose, the more chance there is that some other dame will latch on to him. And I'm not going to have that!

Unfortunately, her willpower was not as strong as her won't power. Twice she "girded her loins" and started up the hill. The first time she made it only halfway before she was struck with an abject attack of cowardice. The second time she made it all the way to the top, only to find Bradley sitting on the porch. "What the hell do *you* want?" he grumbled. And, not having a ready witty answer, Em fled. It was not until almost sundown that she mustered up her courage again, but all her bravery was minutes too late.

As she stepped out the door a Cadillac limousine pulled up in front of her. All her enemies had joined forces and trapped her. Mrs. Colson struggled out of the back seat. Ralph hesitated, clinging to the steering wheel, until a sharp command from the old lady brought him out of the car in a hurry. The two of them confronted her. Not alone, thank God, for Sheba, who had been playing out of sight for three days, must have had some warning, and came flashing up from the barn to stand at her side.

"I think we had better go inside," Mrs. Colson said. She was still the same obnoxious woman, but something was eating at her, bringing more worry lines to her face. What had once been a domineering expression was now a harried look. Her suit hung loosely on her, her blouse was dirt gray rather than immaculate white, and she had picked up a nervous tick from somewhere. Both of them stomped by Emily. She followed them in.

"Do come in," she invited sarcastically. "Could I fetch you a glass of hemlock juice?"

"Don't fool with us," Mrs. Colson said. "We mean business."

"Somebody put on a light," Ralph moaned.

"Don't be silly," Mrs. Colson said grimly. "We want to keep everything in the dark."

"The house is haunted," Ralph insisted. His frail tenor had become a whine. "Don't you keep anything to drink around here?"

"Poppycock," Mrs. Colson insisted. "It's just your nerves. There are no such things as haunts. It's all an old wives' tale. I've lived in this neighborhood for years. There have never been any ghosts, there aren't any ghosts now, and there never will be any ghosts!"

"Of course," Emily agreed. "No such thing. Of course, there *have* been stories. Creatures that rattle in the night. Empty graves. That sort of thing. Nothing either of you would take seriously."

"We're here to talk about Colson Enterprises," Mrs. Colson said.

"So talk."

"You've ruined us," the old lady said. Her shoulders slumped tiredly. "We bought up all the stocks on my son's buy list, and now he isn't buying. The bottom has fallen out of things. I haven't a penny to my name. You are my only hope."

It was growing too dark, Em thought. And they were all ready to be set up, no doubt about it. Now if only she *really* had the power. She would sit back in her chair and summon up half a dozen assorted spirits. And maybe give them both a case of shingles!

"You must surely see by now," Brad's mother began, "that my son is unstable? And yet he holds all the power in Colson Enterprises. We have come to ask you to reconsider your position, Mrs. Sturtevant."

"Miss Sullivan," Em insisted. "I've had a change of heart. Emily Sullivan."

"It doesn't really matter," Mrs. Colson said to her trembling assistant. "I told you there's no use bargaining with the little fool. I want those shares of stock, girl, and I mean to have them now."

"That...sounds like a threat," Em said quietly.

"It is."

Em looked around the familiar little room. There was hardly a tool to defend herself with. "For all you know," she said, "I really *may* be a witch. Did you ever think of that?"

"Nonsense," Mrs. Colson said. "It might frighten rabbits, but not me. I'm made of sterner stuff than that."

"I believe it's possible," Ralph said, almost weeping as he spoke.

"Well, let's see," Em said. She leaned back in her chair and closed her eyes. "Spirits," she chanted, "be heard!"

She waved her hands in front of her, as if throwing something away. And then settled back.

"Ha." Mrs. Colson snorted. "Chicanery."

"Listen." Em put a finger to her lips and shushed them all. From directly above their heads there was a thumping sound, and a moment of silence. And a heavy pair of feet, limping slowly toward the stairs. The crash of a heavy boot, a sliding sound, another crash, a pause.

"You can always tell a practising witch," Em continued in her most mournful tone. "She always has a familiar with her. A cat or a monkey, or something like that, capable of doing terrible things."

"Non——" Mrs. Colson started to say, when a door banged upstairs, and the feet came dragging toward the steps. Ralph almost swallowed his tongue. And just at that moment Sheba darted into the room and jumped up on the second stair. The cat came up on her hind legs and spat at them, stroking with her huge claws.

"I gotta go," Ralph said frantically. "I gotta go to the bathroom." And before another word could be added he fled, running out of the house, down the hill, and into the woods that closed in around the building.

Now, Em told herself, if it were only true. Lean back in your chair. Sheba will come over and sit on your shoulder. She shivered, for Sheba did just that, without a word being said. "The spirits are with us," Em said. "Listen!"

Something moaned at the top of the stairs. Something that could not be seen because of the darkness. "Adelaide," a stern voice commanded, "tell them how I died."

"I don't know what he's talking about," Mrs. Colson said. Her voice had gone up two octaves, and she was clutching the arms of her chair with a death grip.

"Tell them how I died," the voice commanded. "You remember. You were all alone in the room with me."

"I didn't do it!" Mrs. Colson shrieked. "It was all his idea. Ralph did it. I—— Henry? Are you really there?"

"Really there, really there, really there." The voice at the head of the stairs echoed around the empty hall and then faded gently away.

"Get a hold on yourself," Mrs. Colson yelled after the fleeing Ralph. "It's all pure hokum."

Again the voice from the stairs. "Ah, Ralph came too? But now he's gone." The tone dropped deeper. "And wouldn't stay to talk to me? He was there, too, then . . . when I . . . died?" A falsetto voice this time.

Mrs. Colson had half risen, and now froze in position. "I won't forget what you did, and that Ralph helped you," the ghostly voice added. "I'll be waiting here when you both come over. Believe me—Adelaide?"

The words were unheard. Mrs. Colson, despite her old age and high heels, had just taken off like an Olympic runner, through the door, and down the stairs. She stumbled on the bottom stair, which gave Ralph just time to break out of the woods and head for the limousine. Mrs. Colson slid in behind the wheel and the engine churned into furious action.

"Wait for me," Ralph wailed as he came out of the woods. But Brad's mother in the car had had enough. She left him to follow on foot, if he could.

"Oh, Lord," Em said. "I never really thought I had the power!" Sheba chattered at her. The footsteps came thumping down the stairs.

"Neither did I," Brad Colson said.

"Oh, God, Brad!"

"As you see," he laughed. "I saw the pair of them ganging up on you, so I sneaked up the back stairs."

"Oh, Brad." She was in his arms, throwing herself at him. The pressure was too much for a one-legged man. He fell back onto the bottom stair, and Em fell into his lap, frantically hugging him. Sheba, transferred suddenly from familiar to barn cat, came over to check them out, and then headed back down to the barn.

"Did they really... your father?"

"I don't know," he chuckled. "I was away in Britain at the time."

"But you're going to the police?"

"What? Tell them that my mother killed my father? Not me, love. Now, why all this cuddling?"

"I was wrong—all wrong." Em was halfway between laughter and tears. "You were right about Rob. Oh, Brad. I——"

"Forget it," he said as he squeezed her just the right amount. "I thought all along you might have known but didn't want to admit it. And all that ghost business. All part of your overextended imagination, love."

"I suppose you're right," she said, sighing. "But still—for just a moment there I thought I really had the power."

"And you loved it?"

"And I loved it. Brad, what must I do now?"

"I would say, Em, that you ought to forgive and forget, and let's spend another night checking on compatibility. Wouldn't you like that?"

"Of course I would," she giggled at him. "The whole night?"

"The whole night," he agreed.

"And you think you can handle a full session like that?"

"Of course I can," he boasted. "And have enough strength for marriage afterward. Well, almost enough strength."

"Well," Emily said firmly, "you've convinced me that there aren't any ghosts—not a one. I'm so certain of it that if Rob were to walk into the room right this minute I would tell him I forgive him everything!"

There was a brilliant flash of light in the far corner of the room. A ball of light that moved slowly toward them, until it passed them on the stairs. "What the...?" Em muttered. "The apparition again!"

"I don't——" he started to say.

She shushed him with one hand over his mouth. The ball of light stopped, floating in the air above their heads, and then it seemed to expand, flashed upward to the floor above, accompanied by the sound of winds clashing into a vacuum. The sibilant whistle of words was barely audible to her experienced ear.

"Forgive," Rob said. "Forgive," and with that the apparition flashed beyond sight and sound.

"You heard it, didn't you?" She turned excitedly to Brad. "You heard him! He was in that corner..." She gestured wildly. It was only the second time she had a witness.

"Of course," he said. She looked up at him and the smile faded from her face. He was looking in the wrong corner!

"Oh, hellfire and damnation," Emily grumbled. "Don't play games with me. You didn't hear it, did you? You didn't see it, did you?"

Brad wrapped her up tightly in his arms and squeezed. "Honestly?"

"Well, of course honestly," Em said. "I wouldn't want you to lie."

"Then no, it didn't happen," he said. "It didn't happen. It couldn't happen——"

"What are you doing now?" she whispered back frantically. His fingers were toying with the firmness of her breast, and that uneasy feeling was stealing up on her again.

"It didn't happen," he said. "Don't ever tell our grandchildren about this!"

Grandchildren, she thought excitedly. "Are there going to be grandchildren?" That meant loving and marriage and—— "I won't," she whispered in return. She reached over to him to quench that terrible excitement, only to find the feeling was increasing a thousandfold every second. "After all, who would believe me except you?"

"Who knows?" he said, sighing. He buried his face in her fragrant hair. "Maybe Rob will be back some day?"

Em sat up and stared at him. "I'm having a vision," she whispered.

"Oh, God, now what?"

"I have this vision," she repeated. "If you and I don't go to bed immediately—and stay there for a week—all your bones will turn to Jell-O!"

"A week," he chuckled. "That ought to do it, if I can live so long. But just all *my* bones? What about yours?"

"Too late," she giggled as she fell over into his lap. "Mine have turned already!"

WIN-A-FORTUNE
OFFICIAL RULES • MILLION DOLLAR SWEEPSTAKES
NO PURCHASE OR OBLIGATION NECESSARY TO ENTER

To enter, follow the directions published. **ALTERNATE MEANS OF ENTRY:** Hand-print your name and address on a 3″×5″ card and mail to either: Harlequin Win-A-Fortune, 3010 Walden Ave., P.O. Box 1867, Buffalo, NY 14269-1867, or Harlequin Win A Fortune, P.O. Box 609, Fort Erie, Ontario L2A 5X3, and we will assign your Sweepstakes numbers (Limit: one entry per envelope). For eligibility, entries must be received no later than March 31, 1994 and be sent via 1st-class mail. No liability is assumed for printing errors or lost, late or misdirected entries.

To determine winners, the sweepstakes numbers on submitted entries will be compared against a list of randomly preselected prizewinning numbers. In the event all prizes are not claimed via the return of prizewinning numbers, random drawings will be held from among all other entries received to award unclaimed prizes.

Prizewinners will be determined no later than May 30, 1994. Selection of winning numbers and random drawings are under the supervision of D.L. Blair, Inc., an independent judging organization whose decisions are final. One prize to a family or organization. No substitution will be made for any prize, except as offered. Taxes and duties on all prizes are the sole responsibility of winners. Winners will be notified by mail. Chances of winning are determined by the number of entries distributed and received.

Sweepstakes open to persons 18 years of age or older, except employees and immediate family members of Torstar Corporation, D.L. Blair, Inc., their affiliates, subsidiaries and all other agencies, entities and persons connected with the use, marketing or conduct of this Sweepstakes. All applicable laws and regulations apply. Sweepstakes offer void wherever prohibited by law. Any litigation within the province of Quebec respecting the conduct and awarding of a prize in this Sweepstakes must be submitted to the Régies des Loteries et Courses du Quebec. In order to win a prize, residents of Canada will be required to correctly answer a time-limited arithmetical skill-testing question. Values of all prizes are in U.S. currency.

Winners of major prizes will be obligated to sign and return an affidavit of eligibility and release of liability within 30 days of notification. In the event of non-compliance within this time period, prize may be awarded to an alternate winner. Any prize or prize notification returned as undeliverable will result in the awarding of the prize to an alternate winner. By acceptance of their prize, winners consent to use of their names, photographs or other likenesses for purposes of advertising, trade and promotion on behalf of Torstar Corporation without further compensation, unless prohibited by law.

This Sweepstakes is presented by Torstar Corporation, its subsidiaries and affiliates in conjunction with book, merchandise and/or product offerings. Prizes are as follows: Grand Prize—$1,000,000 (payable at $33,333.33 a year for 30 years). First through Sixth Prizes may be presented in different creative executions, each with the following approximate values: First Prize—$35,000; Second Prize—$10,000; 2 Third Prizes—$5,000 each; 5 Fourth Prizes—$1,000 each; 10 Fifth Prizes—$250 each; 1,000 Sixth Prizes—$100 each. Prizewinners will have the opportunity of selecting any prize offered for that level. A travel-prize option if offered and selected by winner, must be completed within 12 months of selection and is subject to hotel and flight accommodations availability. Torstar Corporation may present this sweepstakes utilizing names other than Million Dollar Sweepstakes. For a current list of all prize options offered within prize levels and all names the Sweepstakes may utilize, send a self-addressed stamped envelope (WA residents need not affix return postage) to: Million Dollar Sweepstakes Prize Options/Names, P.O. Box 7410, Blair, NE 68009.

For a list of prizewinners (available after July 31, 1994) send a separate, stamped self-addressed envelope to: Million Dollar Sweepstakes Winners, P.O. Box 4728, Blair NE 68009.

SWP-H493